Praise for *The Fifth of July*

"Gorgeously written and fully immersive, *The Fifth of July* tells the story of the Warners, a family seemingly defined both by their own self-certainty and skepticism of each other. I could feel the salt air, the sand between my toes, the crackle of secrets, lies, omissions, and later, the uncertainty of tragedy. With prose that positively vibrates and characters who defy expectation, Kelly Simmons brings us straight to Nantucket, into the bright, beating heart of this one-of-a-kind family, and never lets us go."

—Kate Moretti, *New York Times* bestselling author of
The Vanishing Year and *Blackbird Season*

Praise for *One More Day*

"Beautifully dark, totally devastating, and so riveting you might find yourself gripping the pages, *One More Day* is about the holes in our lives and how we struggle to fill them, the love of parent for child, and the secrets that define us. Absolutely mesmerizing."

—Caroline Leavitt, *New York Times* bestselling author of
Is This Tomorrow and *Pictures of You*

"*One More Day* is an absolutely riveting book. It's a rare novel that combines intrigue and suspense with so much heart—but that's what makes it one of my favorite new books of this winter."

—Sarah Pekkanen, bestselling author of
Things You Won't Say and *The Opposite of Me*

ALSO BY KELLY SIMMONS

Standing Still
The Bird House
One More Day

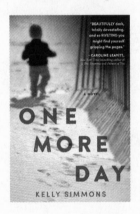

THE FIFTH OF JULY

A NOVEL

KELLY SIMMONS

Published by Sourcebooks Landmark, an imprint of Sourcebooks, Inc.
P.O. Box 4410, Naperville, Illinois 60567-4410
(630) 961-3900
Fax: (630) 961-2168
www.sourcebooks.com

Library of Congress Cataloging-in-Publication Data

Names: Simmons, Kelly, author.
Title: The fifth of July : a novel / Kelly Simmons.
Description: Naperville, IL : Sourcebooks Landmark, [2018]
Identifiers: LCCN 2017014663 | (trade pbk. : alk. paper)
Subjects: LCSH: Domestic fiction.
Classification: LCC PS3619.I5598 F54 2018 | DDC 813/.6--dc23 LC record available at https://lccn.loc.gov/2017014663

Printed and bound in the United States of America.
VP 10 9 8 7 6 5 4

For the Lendways, always.

Matt Whitaker

Of course I held the key.

I hold over two hundred keys, color-tagged, labeled in code, locked in a metal safe. That makes my wealthy clients feel secure, the codes, the locks. I don't mention that my wife also knows how to open it and crack the code. There are reasons for that, practical ones, but clients might not see it that way. Only the beloved, trusted, sober caretaker should have all the keys and all the answers. We don't need to mention anyone else on the payroll or near the safe. Oh, the things I neglect to mention. Like the color-coded tools in my client's own houses, the tiny dot I make so the guys don't toss them into their own trucks. Because things get jumbled in the course of a workday. Some of my guys' trucks are a mess, a tangle of iron and wood, and I don't want anything lost or, yes, stolen. *Stolen*, the word nobody ever wants to hear.

Workers already act like they own the houses; parking on lawns, plunking down Dumpsters, tromping on freshly seeded grass. Washing their dirty hands in a sink that cost three thousand dollars. Pocketing the little soaps or expensive moisturizers for their wives, because there are never any security cameras in bathrooms. These things are not mentioned in the fine print of the caretaking contract or in the hand-shaking assurances I give clients on their porches that cost more than my own house. For their own good, I tell myself. For their own damned good. My clients have other things to worry about, like finding an experienced pilot for their private jet.

Because you know what they say about summer people? Some are people, and summer assholes. It's pretty easy for a guy like me to tell the difference. When you get a call at 10:00 p.m. to go unclog a toilet in a house that has four bathrooms. Or open a window that's stuck. When people are raised with servants, then released into the wilds of Wauwinet for the summer, this is what happens. And then there are the others. The folks who split their own wood, mow their own lawns, trim their own boxwood hedges. They want a caretaker who is more contractor than handyman. These people know where the hammers are, the plungers, the spackle. They don't call you up on a Sunday and ask if you can come over and get a vomit stain out of a white Berber rug.

These are the Warners: Thomas—or Tripp, as everyone called him—and Alice, and their grown children, Caroline and Tom. Plenty of liquid assets, judging from the bills they pay promptly in ten days and the things they don't worry over. But no jets, no nice car. They didn't even have a coffeepot. That's the biggest complaint they received when they started to rent the harbor house every August, the lack of amenities that most people find essential— coffeepot, hair dryer—and I got so sick of hearing that from their tenants year after year, I bought a coffeepot and hair dryer myself and ferried them back and forth from my office. They had all their own tools in the basement, even though I usually used my own. They had lobster mallets and chowder bowls and pots big enough to hold gallons of seawater. They had stacks of wool blankets and row after row of yellow slickers, all sizes and shapes, all salty and sturdy—but they didn't have a coffeepot. Or a microwave or food processor or an electric can opener or, God forbid, a Vitamix.

They were old Nantucket, through and through, and if you don't know what that means, spend a weekend here, and start counting all the elbow patches and Jeep Wagoneers. They're dwindling, but they're not going anywhere. Kind of like swordfish. Decimated, maybe, but not down and out. And my history with all of them aside, they were a kind of welcome relief compared to the mansion owners who couldn't remember the code to their own alarm systems or figure out how to flush their imported toilets.

So when I went to the Warners', I walked in the back door, took off my work boots as I always do, and went through the kitchen in my stockinged feet. Up to the second floor, then the third, and then pulled down the last set of stairs leading to the widow's walk, the metal ladder groaning as it unfolded, then squeaking as I made my way up. After all my years taking care of this house, and all those years before when I was a boy, playing in it with the Warner kids, then dating their daughter, long ago, before she left me, an islander, for guys who probably went to law school or business school—I know those sounds like I know the beating of my own heart.

The first time I kissed Caroline was on the front porch of that house, leaning in tight to the siding, my hands planted against the still-warm cedar planks, June bugs circling the lantern light above our heads. The fog rolling in behind us, the damp grassy smell that warns you the day is changing. The porch invisible to her parents, asleep upstairs, but lit up golden and alive to any boat coming in through the harbor. To the boaters, we would look like a portrait of summer. The houses all alike on this island, soft gray with pale shutters, but this one, different, with us aglow on the porch. They would know it was just the beginning, not the end. That I was on the threshold. That I would kiss her, hidden, forbidden, in every room.

I walk through them, empty, and still feel her faint outlines, her rare smiles, the shadow of her hair. She's as much a part of the architecture as the mullions, the shiplap. Her smell more familiar than salt water and wild roses climbing up a trellised wall. But there's more to it than that, my love of houses. I have a lot of houses. I don't have a lot of Warners. I don't have a lot of Carolines.

I try to tell my wife sometimes how you can know a structure, love it with all its asymmetrical flaws, its broken jambs, its sagging beams, its floors that aren't true anymore but still feel solid underfoot. But I don't think she understands. It's the only thing that makes me get up in the morning, this love of wood, stone, brick, metal. That's how I think of it, not providing a service to the people, but to the houses. I didn't think about my wife or my own house, or the honey-do list Melissa was adding to on the refrigerator. Filling up my weekend with more errands and tasks, filling it so full, there was no time for anything else. Movies, dinner, laughter. Those things were not always on the list.

I pulled on the wooden latch, letting out a square of Technicolor light and a blast of still-cold air. It always seems to be chilly right before the Fourth of July. Like a warning from the universe to not get too comfortable. If I've ever watched fireworks without wool socks, a fleece pullover, and a pair of gloves in one of my many pockets, just in case, I can't remember it. No gloves in my pocket that night, though. No. I had a flask in my vest, as I always do on Fridays. A welcome weight against my ribs, there to remind me that the week is over, and that time and a half is about to begin. You don't mind the intrusions, the constant texts and pings, when you realize how much more they're paying you on a Friday night than a Monday morning.

There were no chairs up there. This was not a porch, a deck, a sunbathing outpost. This was not a room; it was a world. Its own place, separate. You stood tall, away from the warmth of the house, and took the sea wind head on. The Warners' was the highest point on Brant Point, almost as high as houses on the Cliff, nearly as high as the Congregational Church Watchtower, higher than any house has a right to be.

From there, you could see everything new and old. The lighthouses standing firm. The lifeguard chairs, the rocks, the buoys. But also the erosion and the renovations, the wild trees missing, the puny hedges put in their place. Things change in

Nantucket in the blink of an eye. Open a bag of chips, and they go stale in minutes. Salt always clumps in the shaker. Outside, clouds huddle up, then float apart. Water in the harbor is wind-whipped in the morning, millpond in the afternoon. And the homes, built, renovated, torn down to studs, started over. The Warners are in the center, at the heart of all of that newness. They arrive every summer with the smell of sawdust and concrete still in the air. They wake to the sound of hammering and sawing, because the work around them, on their street, in their neighborhood, is never done. A new house, a new porch, a new garage, a new shed, a new driveway, a new mailbox, new new new. And their anger grows with the chorus of all that new each season. I hate being the one to see them drive up every year, as they slow down past every changed house, every overstuffed lot. It's one thing to mourn the loss of a favorite tree or a beloved restaurant. But when a house changes, there's no changing back. Always thought it was funny that they called it "home improvements." There's no improving, usually.

It doesn't always divide that easily for me, though, the love of old and the hatred of new. *New* means work. *New* means people can feed their families. And the fresh cedar, before it goes gray, pale and tender as a newborn's skin. The way the light finds it, holds it. There is hope in those fragile new houses, if you allow yourself to see it, to look for it.

I drank a few fingers of whiskey, leaned lightly on the rail, and watched the sunset spread its pink-and-orange color slowly, extending from Jetties Beach across the water, glinting off the masts and hardware, the goosenecks and pad eyes, painting a shine on everything that holds everything together. In that last half hour after sunset, before gloaming, standing on the highest point, you could not only see the sherbet-orange tint in every direction, you could feel it. It held you in its glowing circle, the trees and church towers and town buildings all radiating. This is how skydivers feel, pilots, snipers. Secret and above it all, three hundred and sixty degrees of fiery sky, when you choose your moment right.

And I always choose my moment right. Not just sunset, but after the subcontractors leave, before the cleaners come to make the beds, a full day before the tenants arrive. Usually anything that can go wrong has already gone wrong. The plumbing checked, the windows cleaned. Not much can happen the next day, in the making of the beds and the last dusting of the fixtures.

I tell you all this so you know that despite all the analyzing, all the nay-saying and fearmongering, all the Monday-morning quarterbacking of what happened next, I wasn't afraid. I went up there myself and thought nothing of it. If you did your homework, if you asked other people on their roofs that day, if you questioned the people coming in to port, standing on the outdoor deck of the Steamship ferry, chilled and full of anticipation, if you wondered aloud if they saw me up there, in my green fleece vest and turquoise wool socks, I'm sure someone did.

I went up there and drank like I owned the place. And that's all.

Sometimes I feel like I own the whole island, that it's mine and mine alone. And none of the other bastards has any claim on it, any right to have it, even a tiny piece.

So add that to your time frame, your theory, your chain of events—add in my fearlessness, my brazen entitlement, my drinking on the job and being paid overtime for it. My proof that of all the things I'm guilty of, that it wasn't me.

I swear to you, it wasn't me.

Not because I didn't want to hurt them all sometimes. Shake them. Knock some sense into them. Especially Caroline. Especially her mother.

But because I would never, ever hurt a house.

Maggie Sue O'Farrell

Every blue moon or so, I get my days confused. Never in July or August, mind you, when it would cost me cold, hard money. But in the shoulder season, when you're getting things ready, it hardly matters whether it's the Grinstaffs on Monday or the Warners on Tuesday. You're just plumping pillows and making beds and putting out towels at that point, just doing a final dusting after opening the house, and you're alone for a change, not working around anyone's luncheon or cocktail party or grandchildren's naps or houseguests who want to sleep in and don't want to find you in their bathroom, scrubbing their stubborn blue toothpaste out of the sink. I don't know what they put in toothpaste nowadays that makes it cling so hard. Rubber? Glue? I use baking soda myself. Spend my day around chemicals, so the last thing I want to do is add some more. No, at home, it's baking soda, vinegar, lemon, and salt. Those four things can shine most anything, including yours truly, who cleans up pretty well if I do say so myself. Run into my clients in town, and they don't even recognize me; clean hair and a swipe of cherry lip gloss and I'm another person. Somebody else, altogether. *See?* I want to say. A little scrub can change everything.

So yes, I was there. Of course I was there. But I didn't go up on the widow's walk, just like I didn't take a soak in their tub or eat clam chowder out of their freezer. Ever since Alice and Tripp Warner moved to Florida from Philadelphia a few years back, they don't open their own house anymore, don't clean their own windows, don't make their own beds. Sooner or later, everyone accepts help, even those two, who made a lifelong hobby of doing chores. She in particular could spend a whole day shining stainless steel and brass, when any sane person would be at the beach with her grandbaby, collecting shells. But it was soothing and artistic to her, somehow, all that rubbing and wiping, like glazing pottery or staining furniture.

Funny how much you can know about a family just by going room to room. You know if they take their rings off before bed or sleep with them on. You know if they're robe wearers or slipper people. If they read at night or watch TV. If they eat in bed. You would be astonished, absolutely freaking amazed, by how many people eat in bed. Or maybe they just do it when they know I'll come by to clean up all the crumbs.

Those are the kind of things you know, but you can't know everything. You might find their diaries, their condoms, their receipts from where they stayed out too late, but you can't see the dark contents of their hearts. I only knew what I'd heard that summer long ago, about Caroline Warner's slumber party; every girl on Nantucket knew the cautionary tale in some form, spun by their mothers, their friends. Details added or taken away, depending on who did the telling and what point they wanted to make. The police interviewed me, but I'd seen so little. Only one boy. Not a whole gang. But that's blended together now with all the old whispers. How it was too cold in the tent out back, the fog seeping through the canvas, how the girls shivered, how Caroline mocked them for going inside. How the boys expected a group of them, giggling in their pajamas, and not one, sleeping and vulnerable behind the delicate mesh and the weak zipper.

But yes, as I told Billy Clayton twice—*twice*—after the accident, and he wrote it down in his little policeman's notepad—of course I know where the Warner family hides their key. Christ on a cracker, I know where everybody's keys are. I also know where they stash the extra toilet paper and cleaning supplies they buy off-island at Costco, and I know every damned plumber and appliance repairman and window cleaner and landscaper and gardener that works on or around Hulbert Avenue. They're basically my coworkers, my coffee breakers. Did I know all the framers and concrete guys who might have been working on the adjacent property, hidden by the tall hedge? Did they see me? Did they know where the key was hidden too? Well, I don't have X-ray vision. I told Billy that also, but he didn't scribble that tidbit down.

That day, I waved to all of the workers and parked my car on the grass since there were two trucks already in the driveway—a detail that didn't seem odd to me at the time, since everybody uses everybody else's driveway when things get tight—and I even spent a good five minutes talking to Chelsea, who was planting hydrangeas across the street. I was yapping away when I heard the sound behind me, the *thwop* of something slamming closed. I turned around but didn't see anything. Looked low, but not high. That was my first instinct: door. But no one was there. I looked awhile too, I promise you that, before I decided it wasn't anything. After all, I was going into a dark house before the family arrived, and even I get spooked now and then.

I went to fish the key out of the hiding place in the bag of mulch (which always creeped me out, to tell the truth; the wet, furry feel of that is grosser than anything I've found inside a toilet the last few years), and I saw Matt in the kitchen.

I went in and said hello, and he told me I had the wrong day. Said it kind of meanly, if you want to know the truth, and not the way we usually spoke to one another. I said I was sorry if that was the case, and he said it *was* the case, and I asked if I should come back the next day instead, and he said no, you're already here.

As if I didn't know that.

"Kind of late, though, isn't it?"

Again, his voice was judgy. Matt liked to be in charge of things a little too much, if you ask me. Power hungry, like his last name was Warner too. *Give it up,* I wanted to tell him. You can tend everything in this house, buff it with your little chamois rag all you like, but it's never gonna be part of you. You aren't like family, no matter how much they say you are. Caroline dumped you a long time ago, and I don't like her, but I sure don't blame her. And you're not my boss; the old lady is. So if she thinks I can clean a house just as good at twilight—then I can damn well clean a house at twilight.

But that's not what I said.

"I had another job," I said, but it was a lie, and he probably knew it. But I didn't owe him an explanation, and I didn't feel like telling him about my doctor appointments, and the last one running late. You had to get all your appointments, all your yearlies, your teeth cleaning, your mammogram, and so forth, out of the way before the summer people descended and your days went all to hell again. I used to pray nothing would happen to me in July or August, no lumps or bumps or nicks or slips. I had a friend waited fifteen hours at Cottage Hospital, bleeding into a dishrag, before they stitched her thumb up, waited while kids came in half-drowned, and young moms burned the skin off their hands boiling lobsters, and old men had heart palpitations on the up and downs of the golf course. No, you want to get sick in the shoulder season, if you have any say about it. Just like you should mostly do your drinking in the winter, but I guess not everybody gets that memo, do they, Matt?

So yeah, when he passed by me, I smelled the alcohol on his breath, but again, I didn't think that much of it. It was Friday, it wasn't the high season quite yet, and he was a man, it was an island. I mean please, what else is new? When he left, the screen door closed softly, with one of those contraptions that keep it from slamming. Then it hit me: the sound I'd heard hadn't been a door. It was the hatch, up on the roof, that opened to the widow's walk. So he was up there, and he was drinking. I was downstairs, and I was sober.

I was there an hour and a half, tops. House looked spiffy—roof patched up tight after the nor'easter; shutters and railings painted white, a soft white, not too crisp. Rockers wiped down, wraparound porch swept clean. The brass door knocker shined up just like the old lady liked it. I did a final once-over, though, top to bottom, since I knew Caroline was coming first, not her mother. She was pickier, more forceful if that was even possible, and the last thing I needed was to piss her off by missing a dust bunny in the corner of her room.

On the third floor, in what the old lady called the Eaves Room, where the low ceiling over the bed could bang your head, there was a series of small family portraits, taken the week of July 4 every year, hung along the chair rail. You could trace the small changes in the family, the rise of their bodies, the fall of their faces. Their hairstyles and tans the same. But anyone could see the difference in Caroline, the before and the after, the small smile that hardened into something else. I straightened the crooked frames, which rumbled every time a truck went down the street, smoothed the quilts on the beds, lowered the window shades to half-mast against the twilight in the harbor, which filled this room, set everything golden and liquid-like. Sometimes it was the hardest room to leave.

Before I left, I always set out two white china plates, two tall white mugs, sugar cubes in a bowl, red cloth napkins folded, not rolled. Big kitchens always looked lonely to me without places set. Later, Billy asked me if I saw anything new or anything unusual that week, and I said, "If I saw something new, that would be unusual." He laughed; he knew what I meant.

That's an old islander mentality—you don't want to add to the landfill. You want to use what you've got until it crumbles. Tourists don't understand, though. When I'm there cleaning early, I've heard them on their early morning power walks. A parade of women pointing at houses midstride, saying what they liked and disliked, as if they were walking through an art gallery and not through a neighborhood of human beings, for God's sake.

They don't say the Warner house is rare, historic. They don't say it's one of the last of its kind. A true summer house, no-nonsense, as many bedrooms as a summer camp, meant to hold three generations. A pull-up-a-chair house. A help-yourself-to-a-drink house. A throw-another-lobster-in-the-pot house.

No. They say, *Oh God, look at that thing. Looks like the porch is tilting. I'd just tear it down and start over.*

I can't even imagine what they'd think about the inside. Nothing in the house was new. Only things with heart, memory, stories woven in. Antique hooked rugs, ancient oil paintings, lace bedspreads so delicate, you didn't dare wash them. I kept the walls free of mold and the simple Quaker furniture free of dust. I made sure the dark, painted floors gleamed underneath the rugs, all of them brightly colored so nobody'd trip. But of course, things wore out. And when they did, they seemed to be swapped with other things in the middle of their life cycle. Broken china replaced with chipped china.

And the old lady had rules, ideas, beliefs about everything. There were no seaside colors in the house like all the other rich people had—no blue or turquoise or coral. The floors were glossy black; the walls, off-white; the furniture, neutral. And there were no whales, no fish, no shells in a glass hurricane, absolutely not. As she once told me: *Shells are for crushing in driveways.* She shuddered at the thought. *Like living with carcasses.*

And of course, along the same lines, no weather vanes, no whirligigs, no painted sign with, God forbid, a name. She named the bedrooms, because there were so many—the White Room, the Front Room, the Dormer Room, the Ladder Room, the Eaves Room. But she hated names on houses. Once, one of their houseguests brought one as a joke and hung it over the porch at night: *Breaking Wind.* I arrived to find her way up on that damned wobbly ladder, pulling it down, half-willing to kill herself before she'd stoop to naming her house. She wasn't afraid of heights, or of taking risks, even as she got older. But she was terrified of tacky, always.

Last year, they came two days earlier than I expected them; I was still sweeping the porch when their car pulled in.

"We came early to go preview the auction," she said, waving the program list in her hand.

"Oh, anything good?"

She knew I liked scrimshaw. Once, she'd given me a bracelet when I helped her get rid of a nest of mice in one of the beds.

"The quarter board from the *Nobska*."

"Whoa, there's a memory for ya," I said. The *Nobska* was the original ferry to the island; I'd thought every piece of it had disappeared long ago.

"Rafael said it would go for five or six thousand dollars, maybe more," Tripp said. "Whaddaya think, Maggie? A good investment?" He winked at me then. That man was a winker. And the nicest one of the bunch, if you ask me. Always smiling with his big, even teeth. Always said hello to me if he saw me in town, greeted me the same way he did his friends.

"Five thousand dollars for a piece a' waterlogged wood," I said, shaking my head.

"Tacky," she agreed and then added, "Things from the water don't belong on land."

That struck me as one of the truest things she'd ever said, right up there with what she told me the year prior, when I pointed out a crack in a bed frame. "If it isn't broken, don't fix it. And if it's just cracked, wait till it's broken."

It was probably that attitude that did the Warners in, in the end. If you ask me. But what do I know? I clean toilets, not solve murders.

Caroline Warner Stark

P ast the jutting rocks of the jetties, inside the harbor, the ferry always slows down, and my heart always speeds up. Anticipation. Dread. I come back every year despite this. Masochist? Maybe. Traditionalist, definitely. I am my parents' daughter, more than I'd care to admit.

Over the years, the anniversary of July 5 had become slightly smaller and more compact, more silvery scar than bloody wound. I was so young, I didn't even know the phrases then. Date rape. Nonconsensual. Witnesses. Corroborate. The language didn't live in us. No one knew how to speak of it. And everyone had their own version of what happened, which seemed to shape-shift over time, even for me. The island could erode anything, bit by bit, year by year. There wasn't a day I ever spent on Nantucket when the rolling surf, the waving sedge grass of the dunes, and yes, even the cloak of fog couldn't paint over, just a little, whatever had happened before.

This year, we'd been summoned early, by my mother, and the sickening feeling in the pit of my stomach deepened. I wondered whether my father was as bad as she'd said. If she was as tired as she'd claimed. It was impossible to picture either of my parents broken. My brother and I? Yes. Them, no.

My father, always athletic, helping us swing a baseball bat, a golf club, a fishing rod. Patient, I see that now, with all kids, not just his own. Like a teacher, he saw the good in kids, even when there wasn't any. Kind, but wrong.

Still, Nantucket is a beautiful place, even when you're hurting. A therapist I went to once, at the insistence of my husband—who means well, dear God, my husband means well—thought my collection of beach glass, mentioned casually, was a metaphor. Beautiful, but in pieces. Once jagged, but getting softer around the edges. *When did you start collecting it?* she asked. The tears threatened at the edges of my eyes, my hands curled into fists. What price would I pay for letting her in, for letting her know? That my childhood was spent collecting shells and rocks, but it changed the summer I turned thirteen. Of course it did. Everything can change when a girl turns thirteen.

My daughter, Sydney, would not be thirteen until October, thank God, and she wasn't one of those precocious twelve-year-olds; she was a younger twelve. Dressed like a boy most days. Still looked longingly at horses, puppies, kittens. That kind of twelve. Some girls stayed that way, I knew. They grew up and became veterinarians, dolphin trainers, zoologists. They could become sailors or rowers. Like me.

I'd learned to swim, to row, to sail, to pilot a boat on Nantucket. My dad taught me, then encouraged me, nudging my way. The path led to my job as a crew coach, starting with hauling skiffs and sunfish on Jetties Beach. Renting equipment, working the sailing camp. I spent all day in a dark-green Speedo, sometimes all night, with a sweatshirt and jeans thrown over it. By the end of the summer, my hair was almost blond, and those tank suits were pale as algae, bleached down, used up. Different in August, always, than I was in June.

I forgot myself, my family, our foibles, in the rise and fall of the waves. And so did the kids I taught. It was amazing how people too young to know their multiplication tables, kids who couldn't read above a fifth-grade level, could be taught to read the wind, the tides, the distance to shore. Some of them just had an aptitude for it. And the looks on their faces when they figured it out, as they tacked back and forth, as it all came about. Shining, proud. Every summer, we found a few who simply belonged on the water, who weren't destined to stay on land. I suppose I was like my father in that way—believing in their goodness, in the possibility of their doing it right.

I was lucky. That first job had shaped me, had taught me, had led me to understanding young girls, to wanting to help them, and yes, desperately wanting to have one. To telling my husband, when I was two months pregnant, that I had to have a girl so I could have a do-over.

So yes, the island led me to everything I have. That it had also led me to things I wanted to shed was almost beside the point.

We were arriving first—to open the house, to get everything ready so my mother wouldn't have to. But also, I knew, to see what was really happening with my father. When she phoned me, Mother said she hadn't slept in a week. She'd had to keep watch over Dad every night; he'd been sleepwalking, going out into traffic, climbing ladders, like he was in some sort of dream state. The chemo had done this to him, she insisted. Rotted his brain, made him half-crazy.

"You mean he's disoriented," I said. I'd read about chemo brain after my friend Cynth, who was a lawyer, got breast cancer. That was her primary fear, not that she'd lose her breast, her hair, but her finely tuned mind.

"No, it's more than that. He's not fuzzy. Some days, he's completely lost the plot. Doesn't seem to know where he is. And taking terrible risks, like going up on the Harrisons' pitched roof just to see the stars. And it's worse at night, when I'm tired. He slips out in the night, wearing dark clothes, and I can't even find him."

"Do we need to layer in some care, Mother? Hire a nurse's aide?"

My parents had insisted I not come to Florida during my father's treatment, that they were fine, that the hospital and visiting nurses had been wonderful, that chemo was boring, boring, boring and nothing to trouble the children with. But of course, I knew: my father didn't want anyone to see him that way. Even family. Even friends. Only my mother.

"He's not disabled, Caroline. He's not diminished. He's…more, not less."

"I don't know what you mean."

"Now that the cancer's gone, he's too goddamned alive!" she said.

"Do you mean…sexually? Is he—"

"Oh, for God's sake, Caroline. Just do as I ask!"

And that was it: we did as she asked. We rearranged our lives, took Sydney out of camp three days early, cancelled John's business trip to North Carolina, and drove all night to get on the next ferry.

My daughter and I stood outside on the boat's deck facing the harbor, watching for seals and sharks and lines of seabirds. A few people walked on the narrow part of the beach; boats bobbed on their tethers. Our house peeked at us in the distance, its widow's walk the tallest point on the street. Legend claimed widow's walks were built to welcome men home from whaling ships, but any Nantucketer knew the truth—they were simply there to help chimney sweeps do their job. My parents had added theirs to the house decades ago to offer a permanent view. Painted it white to match the shutters and stand out from the sky. Our place to watch sunsets and fireworks. A place to see every boat coming in. They usually welcomed us from it, waving towels as we steamed into the harbor. This year, it was empty.

We turned the corner at Brant Point Lighthouse and waved back only to strangers—beachcombers, fishermen in waders casting into the surf—who greeted the ferry, hour after hour, day after day. Year after year. Here we come again. The salt air woke everyone up; the lighthouse made everyone smile. The town dock came into view, the boats gleaming, the lines of families waiting for the arrivals like a parade.

When we were almost docked, we went inside the cabin for our things.

John gathered up the spent cups, spoons, and plates from our snack bar lunch. Sydney ran to the bathroom one last time. The front section of the *Inky*, the Nantucket newspaper John always read before we arrived, was still on the table. I grabbed it to put in recycling, and John put his hand on my arm.

"No," he said. "You need to read something."

"What? Is there some new controversial zoning law forbidding sparklers?"

He pointed to a short news item.

Second Sexual Assault at Steps Beach

June 29 a sixteen-year-old girl reported being attacked by an assailant as she walked home from Steps Beach at 9:00 p.m. The unidentified man, described as over six foot, having a slim but muscular build, floppy blond hair, and wearing a polo-type collared shirt, tackled her and ripped her bathing suit top and cover-up as they struggled. The victim's screams drew the attention of a dog walker above the beach, and when he called down, the attacker fled on foot, running toward Jetties.

Detective Billy Clayton declined to say if this assailant matched the suspect in a similar attack June 14, when a young woman reported being gagged with her bikini top before she managed to get away. When asked if police considered the two incidents to be linked, he said the investigation was ongoing.

For a brief second, I could feel the fear of the girl on the beach, taste the salt and coconut of the swimsuit forced against her clenched teeth. But I shook it away.

I couldn't decide if it was good or bad that Billy Clayton was in charge of the investigation. Still the quiet type. Not giving anything away. I always knew he'd become a cop, but it was hard to picture him grown now, in charge, finally important. At first, I wondered why my mother, who subscribed to the paper and read it religiously, hadn't mentioned these events to us. Then I came to my senses. *Don't believe everything you read* was one of the mantras of our childhood. And my mother wouldn't want to dredge up anything unpleasant during a family vacation. Couldn't fathom raising the red flag over what was probably just hormones at a beach party. I could almost hear her saying that.

"Well," I said, taking a deep breath, "no walking the beach at dark. We don't need to tell Sydney why."

John nodded. "Wearing a polo shirt," he said. "Blond hair. God, it could be anyone."

"They'll investigate a bunch of islanders no matter what."

"What?"

"The girl could have said he was wearing a blue blazer and carrying a Lexus key, and they'd still want to pin it on a local."

He cocked his head, blinked at me. His long, dark lashes could take so very long to blink.

"What do you mean?"

"Just what I said."

"But the police are islanders."

"So?"

"So who is 'they'?"

"This island runs on the money of summer people," I said.

"Even summer people who attack girls on the beach?"

"Yes," I said, my face reddening. I turned away from him as we disembarked, walked briskly, wove through the crowd, the tangle of dog leashes, the bikes.

We grabbed our luggage from the trolley and waited for a cab with all the other families. My brother, Tom, was supposed to be on the same boat, but he'd been delayed, as usual. I watched as other brothers and sisters and cousins embraced, three generations with cable sweaters looped over shoulders. Older men with tanned faces under their bucket hats, all of whom could have been mistaken for my father. Laughing, telling stories, making plans. Soon, they'd have drinks in one hand and the steering wheel of a boat in the other. My mother thought my dad was behaving erratically, taking risks? Please, he'd been taking risks his whole life. Isn't that what drinkers do? Isn't that what islanders do?

As a child, all I saw was that my father was fun, and my mother was mean. At home, I'd wait for him on the front porch like a dog, listening for the sound of his car in the driveway. And in Nantucket? There was not a lot of waiting; he was there, always.

Those late afternoons, when he tried to outrun the enormous car ferry in our little Hinckley boat, cutting across its path in the harbor, heading straight for the spit of Coatue. Tom and I screaming with terror and, yes, joy, as we barely made it, the ferry horn booming in our ears and its tall wake splashing over us, cooling our sunburned shoulders.

Taking us out for walks after dinner so we could stroll through the houses still under construction, climbing high onto plywood platforms, walking up uninspected wooden stairs, swinging from scaffolding like monkey bars. The "don't tell your mother" that was always on his lips.

My mother was never with us on the nights he took us out in the old Jeep, open to the air, stars blinking above our heads, to check on a friend's boathouse in Quidnet after a storm or to fish in the surf at Wauwinet, wherever the stripers were biting. Casting with sharp hooks in the dark while standing in roiling water wasn't dangerous enough, no. After our jaunts, we went for ice cream, driving a specific way back so there was always a moment or two, thrilling in its own way, when he turned off the headlights of the car on the dark twisting island streets, cresting a rise too fast, just to make us scream as the earth fell away.

What I remember most wasn't the menthol of the pink peppermint or the sticky sweetness of the cone. But the bourbon on his breath as he laughed loudly at our protests, half giggles, half cries.

My husband and I believed my mother's warning could have meant my father was drinking even more—combined with meds. And also, just maybe, that something was wrong with my mother. She was tired, exaggerating, suddenly incapable, and she was blaming him. Or had she expected him to die? Prepared for it after his diagnosis, then was disappointed at this new second wind? When I called Tom to loop him in and go over our theories, he suggested that Mom make a video of Dad so we could see. As if my mother could work a camera. As if my mother even had a smartphone.

The cabbie drove through the strip, past the families at the bike shop, past the dressed-up couples at the White Elephant. When he pulled into the shell-lined driveway on Hulbert Avenue, the house closed up tight looked all wrong. Prim and serious. No crooked smile of an open window, no flapping towel on a line, no hum of the outdoor shower. We walked in solemnly, not exclaiming, not sighing, not calling for the dog or wondering what smelled so good in the oven. There was no dinner already cooking, no beach plum crumble cooling on a wire tray, no hydrangeas or wild roses in a vase on the table. All the little homey things my mother would do had not been done. *No signs of life* was the phrase that shot through me and chilled me whenever I thought about it later.

I had been a teenager the last time I'd been at this house when my parents weren't there. When they'd leave for their cocktail party, and timing it perfectly, as darkness fell, Matt would come up the path and slip inside the basement door. The cold earth underfoot, the blanket we kept hidden among the tarps and tents. The blanket I burned after we broke up.

As we walked inside to the sound of no one and the smell of nothing, I felt a shiver run up my spine. *This is what it'll be like when they're dead*, I thought. Sydney ran upstairs, and my heart sank; my mother had always left Sydney a little present on her bed. I should have remembered; I should have brought something for her. I went up after her, hoping to stem her disappointment.

"Mom, look!" Sydney cried.

"Wow," I said.

"How did she do that?"

"Grandmas are smart," I said. But I wondered myself—had my mother outsourced that task to Maggie? Or Matt Whitaker?

Two packages. The first, a Nantucket rope bracelet. The same type of braided circle I'd worn down till it fell off most summers, gray and frayed. She put it on her arm with a smile. Matt probably knew what kids liked on Nantucket, knew from his clients, from observing kids down on the strip, up to no good while their parents shopped and ate dinner. Heck, I thought, he probably knew how to make the bracelets and whipped one up at my mother's request. Matt had always done anything my mother asked, trying to get in her good graces. But that was an impossible task. Didn't keep her from enjoying watching him try, over and over all these years. Keeping him on a leash, using me as bait.

Sydney opened the next package and pulled out a blue tank top edged in small red and gold sequins.

"Wow," she said. "For July 4!"

I frowned. It was tiny, cropped, as if my mother had forgotten how old my daughter was.

"Will that fit you, honey?"

"Yes, it's stretchy, see?"

"Oh, is it a workout top?"

"No, Mom," she said. "It's sparkly! For the holiday."

"Yes, it is. It certainly is."

I had the distinct impression this was an item a cheerleader or drum majorette would wear, but that thought sounded so much like it came out of my mother's brain, I had to squelch it.

I put my suitcase in the green room at the top of the stairs, the one that afforded the least privacy but the most sun. I was always cold in Nantucket. But it was late, and the sun was gone in my east-facing room. It had all moved west, shining upstairs in the Eaves Room. I didn't go up there much, cold or not. When I look at those snapshots, forty of them now, three-by-fives lined up around the room, all I see is what's missing. What I wish was there. To the rest of them, it's just family portraits. To me, it's evidence.

I started putting my clothes away, and so did Sydney. The clank of brass drawer pulls chimed like bells, so loud, I didn't hear John coming up the stairs with the mail, brandishing the single envelope in his hand as if it was good news, a birthday card, a check.

Not a letter from a lawyer, addressed to my father.

I ripped it open without a single thought. John read it over my shoulder, going faster than me, drawing his own conclusions. He put his hand on my shoulder, tenderly, as I was just getting to the last paragraph.

The letter had been sent on behalf of one Robert "Bear" Brownstein, who lived behind us and apparently thought he owned the entire block.

I scanned it quickly, then looked up at John. "What the hell kind of nickname is Bear?"

"Said the daughter of a man named Tripp."

"Not the same and you know it."

"Robert. Rob-bear-t."

"Ugh."

John took the letter, folded it, slipped it back in the envelope for my mother. We'd have to tell her, of course. But I think we both wished we could reseal it and put it back in the mailbox and pretend it wasn't there.

"Someone threatens to sue your parents, and you're wondering about the provenance of his name?"

"It's a mistake," I said.

"The suing? Or the name?"

"Both," I said.

Tom Warner

I gave my sister her own distinctive ringtone on my phone. When Caroline calls, I hear: *trouble trouble trouble*. Because she never calls me unless there's a problem. Never calls to say *hello*, or *happy birthday*, or *I want to set you up with a friend of mine living in Boston*. Nope. When she rang me in June, she was not calling to ask about the weather or my health or my love life. She had an agenda, layered with judgment. That judgment basically just bled through the phone, heavy as a sigh, angry as static. Add my sister to the list of people I continue to disappoint no matter what I fucking do.

I'm sorry, but I can't always do things on her schedule or on my mother's schedule. That's just the way it is when you run a service-based business. My clients call me, or an auction comes up.

Their wine cellar floods, they need replacement bottles. You can say all the time that wine isn't important, isn't a priority, but try telling that to a wealthy client. You work on their schedules, not the other way around. But no one really understands being a wine bitch, except guys like Matt Whitaker. His job, and my job, are really just an inch apart. The fact that I make a shit-ton more money only makes it worse; my clients are that much more demanding, and I have to go to greater lengths to make them happy.

Of course, my family is under the impression that I don't work for a living. Selling wine is, to them, about as difficult as being a golf pro or a lifeguard. *Must be nice. Tough life.* You can't complain when you fly overnight to Paris to an auction, then leave the same afternoon to meet a client in California. No one cares that you are exhausted, slightly hungover, and some days so tired of the word *grape*, the sound of it, the shape of it, that you pick raisins out of the overnight oatmeal the trainer makes you eat and fling them against the wall. No one cares about your shitty fabulous life.

Which is not to say that I don't enjoy it some of the time. Curating a cellar for someone you respect and enjoy is satisfying, fun even. And I still love discovering new blends, tasting something I can't quite put my finger on, a fruit I can't name, layers that unfold. I like a wine that deserves another sip, a second chance.

Anyway, I had to go on standby on the late ferry. I offered to pick up groceries on the way to the house, since I'm bringing my Audi over, but Caroline said no, never mind, in that martyr voice. Just like my mother, doing everything, then blaming everyone else for doing less.

There were lights in the living room and kitchen when I drove up after eleven. No lights upstairs. I thought I saw Caroline up on the widow's walk, and I went to tap my horn but knew they'd kill me if I woke anyone up. I raised my hand instead, but whoever it was didn't wave back. Maybe it was just a shadow, just a trick of the moon.

I left my golf clubs and fishing gear in my trunk; I knew that banging those things up the stairs would just irritate Caroline, whether she was already awake or not.

I walked up the back steps, toward the kitchen, hoping it was John who was up and not her.

In the living room, John was watching a Will Ferrell movie on the flat-screen TV I'd bought last year. I told my parents they had to have one in order to keep the rental price high, and Matt backed me up. But, of course, John and I were both thrilled to have it there so we could watch baseball and golf and tennis, three places where he and I intersected. Sports was our connection, and wine, and cigars, and whiskey. Not the mutual love of my sister, although I'm sure we both loved her in our own way. I just wasn't sure, most of the time, what that way was. She had been a cute kid, always a tomboy. We played together when we were little. But it seems like ever since she was in high school, she's been a stone-cold bitch. Full of attitude and particular about every damned thing, not easygoing like Mom, not amusing like Dad. Just way too fucking grown-up. She was still attractive enough, with her golden hair and skin and her tennis-trim figure. I saw the way guys looked at her when we took walks into town so she could complain about our parents. But I wanted to warn those guys, the same way I should have warned poor John. *Don't be fooled. She'll never let you be.*

"Yo, Bro," John said, muting the movie.

"Don't let me interrupt."

"Please, I know it by heart."

"*Shake and bake,*" I said and laughed. We all knew it by heart. I pulled a bottle of cabernet out of my bag. "Brought you something."

"Ooh," he said. "What year?"

"Before you lost your virginity."

"That recent?"

I smiled. "I'll get glasses. Unless you want to just brown-bag it."

I went into the kitchen and rooted through the cupboards for the decent wine globes I'd bought the year before. Tired of drinking out of my parent's chipped thimbles. Tired of using what was here instead of what was right. It was too much like camping. But it was so, so very Mom and Dad.

We finished the bottle, and I opened another one. We went outside and smoked cigars on the front porch, and that, I suppose, was our first mistake.

A few minutes later, my sister was standing next to us in her Lilly Pulitzer pajamas.

"That shit is wafting through my window," she said.

"Welcome to Nantucket," I said. "Nice to see you too, Sis."

"It's a cigar, not a joint, honey," John said.

"Jesus, you didn't bring that too, Tom, did you?"

"No," I replied. "Would you like to root through my luggage? Maybe do a cavity search?"

John smiled, and Caroline made the scrunched-up face she always made when someone referred to a body part or sex. She actually looked like she could smell the imaginary weed. *Poor John,* I thought. *Poor fucking John.*

"Can I get you a glass?"

"No."

She sat down next to us and proceeded to launch into a schedule for the next two days. *When Mom and Dad arrived. When dinner would be. When we should go out in the boat. When Dad had his therapy. When Mom needed some down time. If I should take Dad fishing. When I should take Dad golfing. When I could meet with Matt to go over the repairs needed on the house.* And whether we needed to go to some kind of township meeting about something or other with our neighbor's lawyer who sent a letter over *blah blah blah blah.*

"Did you hear me?"

"Not really," I said and sighed. John suppressed a cough next to me, which I'm sure he would pay for later, interpreted as a snicker. "Why don't you type up an itinerary and tape it to our doors?"

I knew her next words would be *this isn't funny,* and I was close. So close.

"This isn't a joke, Tom."

"Well, if it is, it goes like this: the good news is Dad survived cancer; the bad news is Mom's gonna kill him."

"Mom needs our help. I don't know if Dad is as bad as she says or if she is just losing it too, but you know the indomitable Alice Fucking Warner would never ask for help unless she was really, truly in the shit."

"Okay, okay. You're right."

"And the new neighbor behind us is building a three-fucking-story quote-unquote pool house and is claiming our widow's walk is out of code and built too high and needs to come down."

"What?"

"You heard me. John has the letter."

"So you're opening Dad's mail now? Mom tell you to do that too?"

"You would have done the same thing."

"Doubtful."

If there was one thing I was sure of, it was that my sister and I did not possess the same instincts about anything.

"Is the widow's walk out of code? It was built so long ago. I think I was in college. Maybe the codes have changed?"

"Who knows?"

"I'm sure Matt knows."

"Matt's not an engineer."

"The widow's walk interrupts this guy's new view," John said. "That's what this is about. Not being out of code. It's about not backing down."

"Well, we have to help Mom with this too. She doesn't need any more to deal with. So you make a tee time on Friday, and you call Matt, and I'll make dinner reservations one night—"

"Okay, okay! But please, let's not go to that stupid place Dad likes."

"What, because you don't like their wine list, we can't go somewhere and have a burger for your father who had cancer?"

"They serve Turning Leaf, Caro. They don't even have a list."

"So drink beer. Suck it up."

"Can we just go to the club?"

"Fine, if you let me drive."

"All right," I said with a sigh. She always thought we drank too much. Sankaty Golf and Beach Club was only a few miles away, but she always made it seem like it was light years. *It's an island*, I wanted to scream. *Everything is around the corner. We could ride our bikes home, for God's sake.*

"If I'd had cancer, I'd want to drink and eat whatever I wanted," John said.

"You *do* drink and eat whatever you want," Caroline said.

"Well, since we're all dying, just slowly, why not?" I asked.

She sighed. "I'm going to bed," she said, but she didn't move.

"Do you want a glass?" I asked.

"Maybe."

John handed her his.

"Wait, did you already brush your teeth?" he asked. "It won't taste good if—"

"I'll live on the edge," she said.

"Ooh, such courage," I said. "Maybe *you* should be the one to call Matt."

"Have you always been such an asshole? Or am I just noticing it, truly, now?"

I stopped to consider this. I thought about my years in lower school, middle school, boarding school. I thought about kicking the winning soccer goal and screaming "Suck it!" I thought about the time I got picked up for public drunkenness and flirted with the policewoman. I thought about hitchhiking and stealing the man's quarters from his ashtray when he went to the men's room. I thought about the friends I used to have who I don't anymore, the girls I dated, the fiancée who dumped me after I got thrown through the plate-glass window of a bar.

"It's possible," I said.

"It's probable," John replied.

She stood up to leave, and I smelled what I've come to think of as her own smell—shampoo and soap and deodorant, all mixed together. Lavender and rose. Not unpleasant, but not sexy, just hers, my sister. I would know it the instant I entered a room. And I wondered if I had a smell. If she could tell where I'd been, if I left a trail as obvious as hers.

"Hey, Caro, were you up on the widow's walk when I drove up?"

"What? No. Put your cigars in water before you come up. You don't want the house to burn down."

"Thanks, Mommy," I said.

"You're welcome, asshole," she replied.

We stayed up late, watching the lights go out, one by one, on all the big houses across the street. You could look in their windows and watch their big-screen TVs; you could practically see the petals on the enormous flower arrangements in their empty foyers. Down the road, catty-corner, the old Grinstaff house had the same sprawling, dark exterior. Renovated twice, and still the arrangement of windows had an unfriendly look to it, no shutters, the pattern of lights inside forming a menacing jack-o'-lantern. But if you stayed up late enough, all the lights went out, even over there.

We talked about fishing, about politics, about business, about everything but family. That was one of the things I loved about John, how he knew not to poke the tender places. The world needed more people like him and fewer people like me, and I knew that. I also knew my sister married him because she thought he would always be on her side, not mine. Shows you how wrong she was.

I stood up, stretched, and looked at all the cars, all the houses, all the boats. Everyone was here waiting for the Fourth. Everyone was in bed, resting up. The summer was just beginning, after all. John said good night, and I went up to the widow's walk with my last cigar. I expected to smell traces of my sister still, the lotion from her hands lingering on the ladder, the hatch, the railing. But there was nothing. Maybe she wasn't lying about being up there. Who knew?

It was too dark to see anything but stars and the glowing end of my cigar. I didn't finish it. After a while, cigars make me feel sick, just like everything else.

Alice Warner

In my memory, which is sometimes as hazy as a foggy beach, the island is a painting in only four colors: gray, white, pink, and green. The gray houses shuttered in white. The tender pink climbing roses. The brighter *Rosa rugosa* freckling the sedge grass that brushed your legs as you ran down to a pearly dollop of private beach.

The people, though... Well, that's all changed. Used to be everyone was someone's friend or brother or cousin or college roommate. The summer people were tethered together like settlers, thirty miles out to sea. Not for us the Jersey shore, the pull of northern Lake Michigan. No. We were willing to go farther, haul more, last longer, to be in a more interesting place. We had that in common too.

People speak of the whaling history of the island, hold it out as its central fascination. Someday, perhaps people will look back at our colonization, our industry, as being more important. The best kind of people, gathered to make the best kind of product: fun.

That has changed. I know change is inevitable, but I hold tight to the idea that a family can still gather, still laugh, still pose for our group portrait the day after the Fourth at the lighthouse. I'd called Earl Greenway to schedule it, and his young camera assistant told me it was already on the calendar. To compare all those photos, throughout the years, lined up, is to see that some things hold fast. Even that one dreadful year, when Caroline's eyes were ringed with red and her face was still bruised from crying, even then, when she refused to stand next to her father or her brother, when she insisted on settling herself at the edge, almost out of frame, we were a family. And this year, even though Tripp looks different and acts different, we will document it too. Even if it's the last year, we'll have a record of it.

Back in the day, Tripp and I used to stay up late, discussing which of our two children was stronger, smarter, funnier, more likely to succeed. This is precisely what children fear, that parents keep everything equal on the face of it—tracking the cost of Christmas presents, doling out equivalent compliments, and then, behind closed doors, discussing them like racehorses.

And I confess: I put my money on Tom. But I was wrong, wasn't I? She is stronger than he is. Just as I am stronger than Tripp. And I wonder if my children did the same calculations, trying to figure out which parent they'd have to bury first?

When Tripp started getting sick, I found four bloodied monogrammed handkerchiefs crumpled in the wash. I walked down the hall to his study where he was filing something or other and demanded to know if he was having nosebleeds. And he confessed that it was just this damned cough, a cough he couldn't shake, and it was nothing. But I took him to the doctor—made his appointment, drove him, followed up with the tests. Because I knew: it was lung cancer.

Caroline lived in New York, and Tom lived in Boston, and Florida was just far enough away to make it a pain for either of them to come down, so we told them not to. They sent flowers; they sent food. (Well, Caroline did. Tom called and left messages that said if we needed anything to just ask. *As if we would ask!*) Tripp didn't want his children watching him getting nauseated or having trouble walking, all of which happened right away.

We soldiered on, prepared to get through it. But the light at the end of the tunnel never seemed to appear. The chemotherapy did something to his brain. Six weeks of it, to shrink the tumor, and shrink it it did. But in its place, an expansion somewhere else. A man's mind in free fall—that's the part no one tells you about, that no one on earth can describe. They call it chemo brain, like mommy brain, like wine brain, like—oh, what do you call it when the kids drink milk shakes?—*brain freeze*, as if it's just temporary. But no. Something seeped into his brain, contorted and squeezed, releasing it into a whole new shape and size. He is a changed man, my husband. It's as if I am living with a stranger.

So there were my son and my daughter, arrived before us, walking up the ferry ramp, each taking a bag from our shoulders. There they were, making small talk as if everything was okay. Tripp was loud, voluble. Did they not notice? He sounded drunk. Shrieking "Caro" and "Tommo" at the top of his lungs.

I stood with Caro near the trolley of luggage, waiting for the rest of our bags, and watched Tripp and Tom take the golf clubs to the car. Tripp walked differently, faster, on the balls of his feet, like an effeminate racewalker. I wanted to take a picture, a video, and go back through it with them, frame by frame. *There it is, right there. The evidence. Don't you see?*

"Dad looks good," Caroline said.

"You don't really think so!"

"Yes," she said. "I wouldn't say it otherwise."

And I thought, *Oh, what a lie that is.* There is nothing worse than an inauthentic person who thinks they are authentic, openhearted, honest. Caroline had always put a gloss on things, said what people wanted to hear, then turned her head away, to hide her cheeks, burning with fury. That blush was the only true thing about her some of those years.

"Caro, look carefully. He's…not well."

"So you say."

"It's true. You'll see. That's why I couldn't let him drive."

"You drove the whole way?"

"We stopped overnight in Connecticut."

"At the Braziers'?"

"No. At a hotel. I didn't want Bob Brazier to see him like this."

"Like what, Mom? He seems completely fine."

I looked to the sky and blinked back tears. I had to save them, I knew, for worse things. I really did know that. I just didn't know what.

"He's *not* fine. Nothing's fine!"

When the luggage trolley came, we each rolled a bag back to the car, where Tripp and Tom stood laughing at something on Tom's phone. Something fluttering beyond them from the streetlight, a handbill of some sort, and it drew Caroline's attention.

I glanced over her shoulder. A crude drawing, a vague headline: *Have you seen this man?*

I ripped the poster off the pole.

"Mom!"

"People can't post things willy-nilly. It's against the zoning," I said.

"Mom, that's a police sketch! They're warning the public about that guy attacking girls on the beach!"

"No one wants to arrive on vacation and see this kind of thing! Now, did you go to the supermarket, Caroline?"

I suppose she had never heard me ask that before. I'd always done everything, after all, short of mowing the lawn, and some summers, I did that too. I certainly knew how to mow a lawn. But caring for an unpredictable adult who weighed 190 pounds? That was proving beyond me.

"Yes, Mom. Everything's ready."

Tripp sat in the front with Tom. He drove his own car, not the island car. Tom always liked things that were newer and nicer than we did. I understand that now; I can't handle the dents and dings. After all these years of living with antiques, I'm changing too: I want Tripp newer, the way he was.

After we moved away from the dock, we drove along the

harbor, past the White Elephant, past Brant Point Lighthouse, the long way along Hulbert that Tom knew I preferred. With all the remodeling of the waterfront homes, every year, the views between properties were diminished to tiny slivers of blue. The only true vista now was from the widow's walk. How prescient we were to build that twenty years ago. Who would know it would come down to that?

Tripp rolled down his window and exclaimed over the sea air, the salt, the smell of roses still floating through. He asked Tom to stop at the Moores' house. He got out, and I wondered if he was going to open the curved wooden gate and walk right across their crushed-shell driveway and make himself a drink, sit out on their porch overlooking the lighthouse. The door was open, of course. All the old gang's were. But no. He went to the split-rail fence climbing with wild roses and sniffed them extravagantly.

"See?" I said to Caro.

"How many times have you told us all to stop and smell the roses, Mom?" she whispered. "Maybe he finally listened to you."

"No," I replied.

"Dad has always liked roses," Tom said. "Don't you remember?"

"No, Tom." I sighed. "No, I don't."

We watched as his father bent over, nose in pink petals, Nantucket reds from waist down to his ankles.

"Well, smelling roses is sweet. And it's harmless," Caroline added.

"Not everything he does is harmless. You'll see."

"Okay, Mom," Caroline said, her voice filled with disbelief and condescension.

"Let's pick some, Alice!" Tripp called from the fence. His smile just a little too wild. "Whaddya say?"

I got out and took his arm. "There's plenty of flowers at home," I said, keeping my voice calm and low, hoping it worked. Sometimes it did. "There are big, blue hydrangeas ringing the porch, remember?"

"Yes," he said, but his eyes were vacant.

"And there's honeysuckle along the public way to the beach. You can smell it when you sit out and have your tea."

"Yes."

"And later, we'll walk down to the beach, and there'll be star grass and chokeberry."

"There are roses in 'Sconset," he said suddenly.

"Yes, where your parents lived, everyone had roses climbing up their cottages; that's right. And on the Polpis path, you could see bayberry and all kinds of other things too."

"And poison ivy," he said suddenly. "Damned ivy."

"Yes, but beautiful things too," I said, as if it were a good-night story, and a happy ending had to be emphasized.

I got him back in the car, and he started planning a fishing trip with Tom. I took a deep breath. The thought of him in the boat, in waders, water over his head, hooks near the fleshy parts of his hands, made me ill. The worrying came back to me all over again. It was like having a toddler, the constant concern, the visions of falling, the impending doom. I looked at the crumpled paper in my lap. Tripp could run away, go deep into a wave thinking he could surf. And then I suppose we'd have to post a sketch of him. *Have you seen this man too?*

It has begun, I thought to myself.

The slow drowning. The unraveling. The beginning of the end.

This, I think, is why people always say they want to die in their sleep.

So they don't see it coming.

**FROM THE DESK OF LIEUTENANT
BILLY CLAYTON**

Call from Steamship Wharf, Report of Police Sketch
Removal, June 28, 2017

Female caller wished to remain anonymous

Indicated that someone on their ferry tore down
sketch of suspected assailant

Described as woman in her seventies with chin-
length gray hair, pale-blue sweater, and white
jeans

Apologized and admitted that didn't exactly narrow
things down

Maggie Sue

Yes, I cleaned the Brownsteins' house and the Grinstaffs' too. After the accident, everyone made a huge deal about that, as if I was the lynchpin somehow, the glue to every bad thing that stuck to that family. How did that happen? Exactly the way you think it would. Bear Brownstein saw me at the Warners' back in April, about six months after he'd bought the house. I did one of the Warners' twice-yearly big cleanings that month, beating rugs on the porch, airing things out, telling the window cleaners where they missed a spot, and he came over and said it looked like I knew what I was doing. And I said, "Well, I ought to. I've been doing it for twenty years."

"It can't be easy keeping *that* house clean," he said then with a kind of sigh.

"What do you mean?"

"Well, so much stuff. All of it old."

"Well, when it's clean, it feels newer."

"That's an excellent attitude."

"Thank you," I said.

I'd stopped beating the rugs, because the dust would have gone into his face. He looked out of place on the lawn, framed by the blue sky and the blue water, in his black blazer and jeans and black T-shirt. Like he belonged in New York, somewhere dark, without all that blue behind him. Not that I'd ever been to New York. No desire. I can see skyscrapers and Broadway shows in Boston or even Providence.

"How much would you charge to clean an easier house?"

I laughed. "I charge by size, not by quote-unquote ease. And if your house is the one I think it is, it's very, very big."

"Well, that seems backward."

"It's the only fair way to do it."

"Wouldn't hourly be the fair way to do it? In the city, they charge by the hour."

"Well, we're not in the city," I replied. "And out here *on an island*, if you buy me for three hours, trying to save money, you'll be unhappy, because parts of your house won't be clean. You know what I mean?"

"If there's less furniture, and fewer knickknacks, and smoother surfaces, and only one nice, very clean person living in it, you should be able to clean a house in three hours."

"How do you know? You ever try to clean your own house top to bottom?"

He laughed, and that made me smile. He could dish it out, and he could take it, and really, what more could you ask for? People around here claim that New Yorkers are different from people from Boston, Philadelphia, the Midwest. Buying up the houses, adding on crazy things like wine cellars and gift-wrapping rooms and fancy basements with pool tables that'll just get ruined with the first nor'easter that comes through. All that Wall Street money and no good old-fashioned sense. But I didn't see that with him, not at all. He was modest, clean, kept to himself. So I started working for him. Fit him in the next day, early, from 6:00 to 10:00 a.m., since he said it didn't matter how early I began. I liked that about him too, his flexibility.

And yes, I liked him in a way, but I hadn't met his family yet. When you start cleaning a house, you aren't cleaning for one person but a group. And there are always different people in that kind of lineup, like a committee. Someone who bugs you. Someone who mistreats you. Someone who spills hairspray all over the wooden furniture and then blames the house cleaner. Someone who claims a ring was "stolen" when they really misplaced it. The whole Brownstein clan was coming up in August, and there was a wedding planned for his daughter. And that's about all I could say about things.

And yes, you can get to know a family through their home, their belongings. It takes time, and sooner or later, you stumble onto harmless secrets, like a dildo in a drawer, and some not-so-harmless ones, like Tom Warner's bourbon hidden in the laundry cubby. And it's easy to see what people are like on the surface: Do they love needlepoint? Do they hunt deer? Do they paint watercolor? And unfortunately, you do become intimate with their menstrual cycles and their stomach issues. I can spot irritable bowel syndrome at ten paces, my friends. But Bear was there alone, and he was right—he owned hardly anything.

Call it modern; call it minimalist. His living room in the main house—I'd never cleaned in the pool house, because it was being renovated, and he thought it was a waste to clean something that was going to be demolished—was furnished like something out of a men's magazine. Nothing feminine in the whole place. A tall wall of bookshelves with one of those library ladders. A low credenza, two gray sofas that barely had arms or backs. A chrome bar on wheels that held glasses and wine and needed to be dusted. A sheepskin rug, which seemed ridiculous at a beach house. It would be the hardest thing to clean in the whole house if someone spilled on it. There was nothing in the credenza, only a few photographs on the walls. In the corner, a sculpture of what looked like a clothespin, which he told me never to clean because it was too risky.

"I guess you don't have grandkids," I said, and he laughed.

"Don't rush that. I'm only fifty," he replied.

I didn't tell him I was forty and had two. The less he knew about me, the better.

His bedroom had nice clothes hanging in the closet, beautiful wooden hangers. No curtains, only thin linen shades that were too complicated for me; they had their own remote and moved in multiple directions. I just left them be.

So yeah, I made a few beds. I vacuumed; I dusted. His bathroom wasn't messy at all; it made me wonder if he worked at an office somewhere and didn't spend much time at his house. He was hardly ever there when I was there. Even at 6:00 a.m., he was gone or on his way out, and I preferred that, I did. And he left me cash, always. No checks. I preferred that too.

So all in all, I liked him. I wish all my clients were that clean, that flexible, that cash-heavy, and that *gone*. There was one car in the driveway, always—a Range Rover. Maybe he had a second car. I never saw a bike. Billy Clayton kept asking me where he walked, and it was hard to imagine him walking along the beach in blue jeans and a blazer. Easy to imagine him in a restaurant or bar. But he didn't drink. I never found a wineglass or old-fashioned in his sink or his dishwasher, and all the wine bottles on his bar cart were dusty, for show. There was none in his refrigerator, no wine cellar, wine refrigerator. No bottles in recycling. Billy Clayton looked disappointed when I told him that too. What did he hope for? A drunk man who snuck around on foot, spying on all his neighbors, plotting revenge? Some kind of crazed real estate magnate who wanted to skirt the historic society and buy all of Brant Point?

What more did they want me to tell them? He lived simply; he seemed uncomplicated. If you asked me to guess what he did for a living, I would say accountant. Or a librarian who inherited a lot of money.

They were looking for evidence of the crimes, yes—lawn mowers, axes, ladders, gloves, accelerants—but also something darker, harder to pinpoint. They wanted to believe he had a black heart. And how do you find that? What do you search for?

It's not that I didn't snoop, didn't open a drawer or a closet or a cupboard. Of course I did. It's part of the job, to know what's where. Not because I care what they own, but because I need to inventory, I need knowledge, in case I'm accused of anything.

And sometimes I thought that was where Billy Clayton was heading. Dancing around questions about my houses, heading toward questions about me. Where I was July 4, and not what I saw.

But I know this: building a home and following the law and pointing out when someone else was breaking it was not a crime. It was being a good citizen, not a bad one. I know I'm in the minority on this, but I don't care.

I clean 'em as I find 'em.

I call 'em as I see 'em.

Caroline

D ad seems fine," Tom said the next morning at breakfast. My father was out on the porch, arguing with my mother, his voice increasing in volume as hers lowered. They'd been up for hours; I'd heard them squabbling in the hallway, the bathroom, the kitchen, and now the porch. When I came down to the kitchen, he was trying to tell her that she was making tea the wrong way. As if my father had ever boiled water. As if he actually knew where the tea bags were.

"Tom," I said and sighed. "Can you hear him out there?"

"The beach is boring, Alice!" Dad cried through the window. "That's why we should all go kiteboarding after golf! Or Rollerblading!"

"He's just antsy."

"And you're just deluded."

"Since when do you agree with Mom all the time?"

"Well, this time, she's right."

"He'll feel better out on the golf course this afternoon."

That was the Warner recipe for setting things right—fresh air and exercise. Every day, no matter the weather. At college, my roommates were horrified when they learned my mother let us play outside during thunderstorms. Encouraged it. Insisted on it. How she told us lightning was only dangerous if you were in water or climbing a tree. Soccer, baseball, tag, or monkey in the middle? Perfectly fine activities for a thunderous backdrop.

My father and mother came into the kitchen, and Dad clapped his hands.

"Who wants to go for a bike ride? Tommo? Caro? Whaddya say?"

"No one," I said quickly. "We're...busy."

"You don't look busy," Dad said. "And the day's a'wasting!"

"Well, Tom and John were just leaving to go to the neighbor's about the...*thing*," I said, raising my eyes. "And Sydney and I are going to go bring up the coolers and picnic blankets from the basement for later this week. You can help us, Dad."

"The thing?" My brother rubbed his eyes.

I grabbed his arm and whispered roughly in his ear, "The letter. The widow's walk."

My father started doing jumping jacks in the middle of the kitchen, his sneakers squeaking with every leap.

"Maybe I should go with Alice to the neighbor," John said. "And Tom can help Tripp with the coolers."

"Wait," Tom said. "Am I going to the neighbor or going to the basement? You know, because I'm not a grown man in charge of my own destiny. Besides, the neighbor's not here. No car, no lights."

I sighed. "Tom, go down in the basement, and get the ladder while you're there," I said. "The lightbulb at the top of the stairs is out."

"I'll do that when I get back," John said.

"No! Dear God, let him do something for a change!"

"Jesus," Tom said. "Sydney, can you please take Pop downstairs to get the coolers while I talk to your grandmother?"

Sydney shrugged and followed Tripp downstairs. My mother stood nervously at the top of the steps and watched them descend. I believed she was right; there was something wrong with my father. But I didn't think he had to be watched like a hawk every second of the day. Surely we could trust him for short stretches? But the look on my mother's face told a different story. And then it hit me:

she had never worried over me like that. I'd never seen that look on her face.

"Mom," Tom said. "How well do you know the neighbor behind us?"

"Which side?"

"There's only one side. A man named Brownstein bought both properties."

"Oh, right. Him. All I know is that he's Jewish. But I don't think I've seen him."

"Well," John said, "he's seen us. And he's not finished."

"What on earth do you mean? You're talking in code."

"He's planning a huge build—a pool house."

"A pool house?" My mother reacted as if we'd told her he was planning a whorehouse. "Who would do such a thing? There's no room for a pool! Who needs a pool when the ocean is across the street?"

I sighed. There were two properties on our side of the street with pools—using two lots each on both sides of the street, shielded with tall landscaping. All the construction disturbed my parents— I'd watched them sit on our porch and shake their heads, reacting to the expansion across the street, to our ocean views being gobbled up slowly, year by year, by garages and sheds and cupolas and trees and hedges, and it had been heartbreaking. And my mother didn't even realize what my father had done two Octobers ago—poisoning the neighbor's tree that had spread into the last inches of waterfront viewing from the right side of the porch. The tree died—and the neighbors promptly installed a video security system, which looked almost as hideous from the street as the out-of-proportion tree.

"Good God," my mother said. "The sound of it alone will be horrific. The splashing, the screaming. Not to mention the smell. I'm sure he won't have the sense to have a saltwater pool. I'm sure he's a *chlorine man*."

"Well, he's a man with a lawyer. Who claims our house is out of code."

"Our house? He's building a pool and a pool house, and somehow we are the problem?"

"He says our widow's walk is three feet taller than the code allows."

"Well, we can't take it down. It's the only view we have!"

"Well, that's the thing, Mom. Does he realize that? Do you think this person understands the implication of this?"

"I'm sure he does not."

"So he's never been here?"

"No, he most certainly has not!"

"Well, not that we know of," Tom said.

"What does that mean?"

"Come on, guys," he replied. "Security is not exactly tight here at Casa Warner. Half the island probably knows where the key is hidden."

"They do not!" my mother said. "We change the location every so often, and we only have a few people—"

"Do you really think Matt Whitaker comes over here every time to let the subcontractors in himself? Every time a window is washed, or a plumbing leak is fixed, or a refrigerator repairman comes—" I said.

"Yes," my mother said. "Yes, I do."

Tom's eyes met mine. Of course she would believe that, would believe that Matt Whitaker would do anything for her, to try to win her over, still. And part of me believed she was right; Matt was a by-the-book kind of guy. Unless Tom knew something I didn't know. He was his friend, not mine.

"How would this Brownstein guy have gotten the exact measurement?" Tom asked. "He didn't see the plans. He'd have to be over here to do that, to get it surveyed, whatever."

"Or have someone on the inside," I added.

"Listen to you," my mother said. "That's impossible. It's just an estimation."

"Is it, Mom? He knows too much. Maybe we can prove that he trespassed."

"This is all ridiculous," my mother said. "We'll just go over there and talk to him, like a reasonable person would. There is no need for him to do anything, to call for an investigation or whatever—"

"It's a hearing, Mom. In front of the housing committee."

"When is it scheduled?"

"Next week."

"So you'll have to stay then."

"Well, we could get it rescheduled maybe—"

"Or Matt can go."

"Actually," John said, "that proves that maybe you have a shot. If this guy was really an asshole, he'd get it scheduled for the off-season, to ensure you wouldn't attend."

"It's simple: we'll invite this gentleman over for cocktails on the widow's walk," she said. "He'll see that it's our lifeline, and he won't take it away from us."

"Okay, Mom," I said and sighed.

"I would call a lawyer anyway," John said.

"This is silly, even discussing it," my mother said. "There will be no need for lawyers among civilized people. Now, shall we have a little lunch before the boys go to golf?"

"Yes," I replied. "There's turkey and ham and fresh bread."

"Is there soup?"

"Soup?" It was seventy-eight degrees; I had not bought soup. I had not made soup.

"Your father likes soup."

"He does?"

"He does now."

"He can get some at the club," John said.

Downstairs, we heard a crash, and I ran to the basement door.

"Dad!" I cried, but all I heard, in response, was giggling. Two sets of giggles, one young, one old, and they sounded damned near identical.

"Lightbulb," I said to Tom as I went upstairs to change.

"Yes, Commandant," he said, clicking his loafers together.

Tom

We took the Jeep, Caroline and John in front, and Dad and I flanking Sydney in the back. The plan was for the guys to golf and the girls to swim at the beach club, which was about a mile away from the golf course. The 'Sconset side of the island was beautiful but not for the faint of heart this early in the season. Windier, cooler, cloudier. High waves, ragged eroding cliffs. Sydney and Caroline might have to rappel to get down to the beach.

My father was definitely animated on the drive. He'd always been outgoing, but now he was…loud. He shout-sang along to the radio, trying to teach Sydney the words to Sinatra songs and then to get her to sing harmony. It would have been a simple, sweet multigenerational moment except for one thing—my father had never been able to carry a tune. Now, suddenly, he had volume, pitch, confidence. I felt like I was listening to someone else.

"Dad," I said. "Have you been taking…singing lessons?"

"Singing lessons?" he cried. "Oh, that's a good one. I'll have you know your mother would never let me spend money on something like that. She won't even buy fresh onions. She uses onion powder."

"Dad, that's not true."

My mother loved farmers markets, picking up produce, inspecting everything, bargaining.

"Yes, it is. She's…she's changed," he bellowed. "She's no goddamn fun anymore! No sense of humor, never wants to go anywhere, and never wants me to drive, ride a bike, or go skateboarding."

"Skateboarding?"

"Well, technically, it's a hoverboard."

Sydney's eyes widened. "You have a hoverboard? Courtney has a hoverboard!"

"Well, Courtney sounds like the gal for me! Is she married?"

"Pop, she's thirteen!"

"Well, she sounds perfect. What's she doing this summer? Can she fly over and spend the Fourth with us?"

"Dad," my sister cautioned.

"I could ask her," Sydney said, her voice practically thrumming with excitement.

"No," Caroline said.

"But Pop said—"

"No."

"It's my house," my father said.

"Yeah, Mom, it's his house!"

I rubbed my head. "So, Dad, when did you take up hoverboarding?"

"Oh, I don't remember, but it's fantastic, Tommo. Have you tried it? Have you? Huh?"

My father's eyes are naturally large and expressive, dark blue and long-lashed, even now, when gray hairs have wormed their way in. And that day, they grew even wider and larger, childlike. My mother had already told us he wasn't on any medications. But something about the way he moved reminded me of one of the older bodybuilders I'd seen at the gym. Was he taking testosterone or Viagra, something one of his buddies told him about?

"No, Dad, I have not."

"Let me try and describe it. It's like flying. It's like…it's like… um—"

He was practically bouncing up and down in the car. As if he was going to lunge forward and grab the wheel.

"Dad, that's all right. You can tell us later—"

"No, I'm just searching for the right words because it's like nothing I've ever done before! Not skiing, not—"

"It's kind of like snowboarding," Sydney said. "Without the snow."

"Well, now, I've never gone snowboarding! Maybe we can go this winter!"

"So where does one hoverboard? On the lawn?"

"No, Mom, on the pavement."

"Dad, you are not seriously considering hoverboarding on Hulbert Avenue."

"No, no, your mother won't let me anymore. We had a huge dustup over it, and she threatened to leave me."

"So you didn't bring the board."

"No."

"Aw, man," Sydney said.

"But Courtney could come and bring hers!" he said, twinkling.

"Yes!"

"Courtney is not coming to Nantucket!" Caroline said with a sigh.

Could this just be a very, very late midlife crisis? Mom said it was forgetfulness from the chemo. *He's forgotten how old he is*, she'd said. And I'd thought, *What kind of monster would ever complain about chemo saving their husband's life and making him feel young again?* But I had to admit: Dad's energy was, at minimum, exhausting. Especially on five hours of sleep and a wine headache.

"Dad, could we just focus on the one sport, golfing, today?" I said.

"Okay. And tomorrow, we'll go hang gliding!"

We pulled in to the golf club entrance. The click and clack of golf cleats on pavement, then the loud flapping of flags on the greens. It was blowing hard, offshore.

"You can play nine instead of eighteen," Caroline said as she tried to tie back her hair. "We'll come back for you in a couple of hours."

"Oh, hell no, Caro. We're used to wind. Wind doesn't bother a Warner!"

"Don't drink," Caroline said to John as he closed the door.

"We won't," he replied.

"Speak for yourself, buddy," I whispered to him as I picked up my dad's clubs and headed toward the carts.

Alice

The best part of Fourth of July on Nantucket is the way the whole island *agrees*: the world simply must turn red, white, and blue. I love seeing the flags flying, the buntings, the store windows decked out. And then, on the actual day, the boys in their navy-tipped Ralph Lauren sweaters and their Nantucket red shorts. The girls in their star-sprinkled dresses. The dogs with their scarlet kerchiefs. Oh, the island does up Daffodil Weekend with yellow and white, and Christmas Stroll with red and green, which we occasionally came up for, but there's nothing really as festive as the Fourth. It's one of the few days I don't really mind how crowded the island gets; more people just means more streamers on bicycles, more families dressed identically, more sparklers twirling in tiny fists, lighting up the night.

There was plenty for me to still do at the house, though I didn't want Caro to know that. She simply doesn't understand the rhythms of keeping a second home, and there's such a difference between raising one child and two and having a husband who helps. Caro really doesn't know how to run a big house on her own, how to manage a big life with many moving pieces.

I started by making two blueberry pies and a raspberry cake and putting them to bake. Then I got out the navy-and-white anchor pillows from the linen closet and perched them on the white rocking chairs along the porch. I cut some blue hydrangeas, mixed them with poppies, put them in vases. And I pulled the flag out from the attic, beat the dust from it, and unfurled it in the flag stand.

There, I thought, standing on the front lawn admiring my work, the scent of buttery crust wafting through the open windows. All I needed was a red geranium hanging basket from Bartlett's, and I was ready.

"Nice pillows," someone said behind me.

I turned.

A man with dark, floppy hair walked up the narrow strip of grass that separated my house from the Lamberts' next door. That's what I remember most clearly—the length and sheen of his hair, like a dog's coat. Not human. He didn't look like he belonged to our species even, let alone our island. But that was just an impression, a feeling, a twinge-in-my-gut kind of distaste. I suppose I like a certain kind of man, who looks like a man. Who doesn't apply products to his hair, who doesn't mince about with it, who doesn't trespass on other people's lawns.

Still, one thing was for certain: he wasn't a Lambert and wasn't a Warner and wasn't wearing anything that even closely resembled work clothes. His shoes, as I recall now, were camel suede. Ridiculous choice when you lived near the water.

"Can I help you?"

"No," he replied and kept walking. I moved to the driveway and watched him, expecting him to turn to the right and go behind the Lamberts' and proceed to do something that explained it all—brandish a yardstick or pen, or take photos of their back porch. He could be an architect, a real estate agent, an artist sketching the house. I continued, despite my distaste, to give him the benefit of the doubt. But he did none of those logical things. Nor did he turn right.

No. He started whistling, loudly and off-key, a show tune I couldn't place, and kept walking on that tiny slip of grass that the

Lamberts always mowed, that I'd always assumed was on their property though it abutted our driveway, and kept going past the back corner of my yard and the Lamberts', toward the hedges, where he reached out and split one with his arm. It bent easily, softly, allowing him access, and then sprang back. He disappeared as quickly as he'd appeared.

Then I realized. This was *him*. Bear Brownstein. The neighbor in back who sent the letter! The coward! That he could have walked right by me and not said a word!

I followed in his footsteps, down the strip, back to the hedge, then cast about for the same place to open and walk through. Finally, I found it, the soft bendy growth, and I ducked down and went through the other side.

It had been a year since they'd brought in the eight-foot hedge, marking their now-oblong property as clearly as a fence. I wasn't a fan of boxwood—I considered it prosaic and overdone—but the explosion of wildflowers in his flower beds was breathtaking, really, and for a few seconds, I wondered who their gardeners were, and who had designed this, and whether I could do something similar in the bed on the other side of my house. Then I came to my senses and realized the man was gone. Was he in the main house on the right, the renovated one? Or the old potter's cottage to the left, boarded up? Or was I wrong, and he'd cut through to another house?

I knocked firmly on the door of the main house. Took him a few seconds to come to the door, and when he did, he said "Yes?" right through the screen.

"Mr. Brownstein?"

"I am."

"I'm your neighbor to the north, Alice Warner."

"How can I help you?"

I smiled as broadly as I could under the circumstances. It almost hurt my teeth to do so.

"Well, we'd like to invite you over for a cocktail. Perhaps tomorrow?"

"I don't drink."

He said this proudly, as if he thought it distinguished him somehow. And it did certainly mark him in my eyes. After all, who can trust a man who doesn't drink?

"Well, a lemonade then, and we can discuss your letter—"

"No thank you, Mrs. Warner."

"No thank you?"

"There's nothing to discuss. Now, if you'll excuse me."

And then he was gone. Without ever opening the door. Without so much as shaking my hand, let alone drinking my drink or eating my cocktail peanuts.

I turned on my heel and pounded down his porch stairs. Maybe it was time for me to write him a letter! Outlining his rudeness, his sense of entitlement, his boorish habits of not opening doors and not shaking hands!

As I neared the edge of his property and kept my eyes peeled for the opening in the hedge, suddenly, with nary a warning, sprinklers started coming on, one by one, in a kind of formation. The first sprays hit me chest-level, and then, arcing, on my head, shoulders. He may as well have turned the hose on me directly!

Now I know some of these systems are wholly automated, timed for the cool of the afternoon, but that was hard to believe, in the moment, as I stood there half-drenched. Part of me remembered the freedom of running through sprinklers when I was young, the squish of grass between my toes, the rivulets dripping off the cropped edge of my hair. Another person would be far more disturbed by this cool spray of water than I would.

But then it hit me, harder than the water. A message.

I can walk on your property but you can't walk on mine.

That realization fed my fury, not the water. I marched right back to the front door to tell him I'd see him in court! That I would not back down! A drowned gray rat of a woman who would not hide behind a letter or statute!

I tried the door; locked. I jimmied the window; locked.

And what does that tell you about his character? I mean, who on earth locks their doors and windows in broad daylight in Nantucket?

Whoever he thought he was, wherever he believed he was hiding, I hope he was thinking something similarly about me: Who on earth barrels through a gauntlet of cold water to break into an enemy's house?

Me, that's who.

Water doesn't bother a Warner.

Tom

O n the golf course, I always turned off my phone, but I could still sense the alerts, the messages, piling up. Like a child tugging on your hand, insistent. Some vacations, I spend half the time on the phone, being that guy everyone hates.

This same time last year, Dad and I had played Sankaty as a twosome; John stayed home with Sydney. Then the chorus in my pocket began. *Ping ping ping.* We were on the fifth hole nearest the lighthouse, and I told my dad I had to take a walk and answer some of these texts. Dad had frowned and said that he'd wait for me by the lighthouse. I hadn't gone more than a few steps when I thought to glance back. Why I turned back, I don't know.

Still, I didn't run. Last summer, we didn't know *anything*. Didn't even know he had cancer yet. It was late in the afternoon, and the sky had that liquid quality that made everything look better than it actually was. My father stood at the base of the lighthouse, dug in his golf bag, pulled out a tool that glinted in the light.

"Dad!" I called, but he didn't turn. "What are you doing?"

"They were supposed to leave it open for me!"

"What? Who?"

"The guy I tipped."

"Who, Dad?"

He gripped the wire cutters, snapped the chain link in two, neatly.

"Jesus, Dad, you can't—"

"Sure I can," he said and winked. "The amount of dues I pay? You bet I can. Plus your mother is the head of the membership committee. She won't vote her own husband off!"

He opened the door and went in, started up the stairs, then turned back.

"Well, are you going to stand there or come up and enjoy the view?"

We climbed up. Afterward, I would wonder what else he kept in his golf bag—zip ties, knives, if my father was some kind of country club criminal. But that was later. I followed him to the top, to the highest point on the bluff, and looked across the streaky turquoise sky. Did he see something coming? Whitecaps, sails, seals? He looked the same way he had on our childhood jaunts up to Altar Rock or Gibbs Pond, the shimmering blue pond tucked deep in the moors, a place for islanders, mountain bikers, hikers, not tourists. How he used to marvel at being able to see in all directions, without having to see people. How proud he was that no one else could see what he saw.

I hadn't told anyone about that incident at the lighthouse, but now my mother's concerns rattled in my head. Before I loaded my father's worn golf bag into the Jeep, I rooted around in the pockets, looking for tools and sharp objects, but all I found was an extra crumpled glove.

The day started out fine. John missed a putt by a half inch, and we all stomped on the green, trying to get it to roll in, then laughed at our collective inability to do so. Dad wasn't agitated when he lost his ball in the rough two shots in a row. That would have set another person off, but he was jolly. And no one was upset when I stepped away to take a phone call from Matt Whitaker. I'd left him a message, saying it was important. He said he'd do a little digging and get back to me as soon as he knew anything.

The foursome behind us was Kip Moore and his three sons-in-law. Kip asked us if we knew anything about our neighbors, who were up for membership vote. *Brownstein* was the name, he said with an arched eyebrow. John and I exchanged glances.

"Never met the man," I said evenly.

"But he lives behind you."

"He's never on-island."

"Hmm," he said. "They prefer members who will use the club, play an active role."

I shrugged.

"And of course they prefer them to be Episcopalian, but you can't say that out loud anymore, can you? God damn political correctness, right?"

I nodded. I knew better than to get into a debate with someone my father's age about religion, Ronald Reagan, or Fox News.

We urged Dad to play a little faster, since the Moores kept coming up behind us, and they were too polite to play through. And then, well, we let him drive the cart. Seemed harmless enough until he chased a bird, pulled the wheel too sharply, tipped it over. Afterward, he made a big scene at lunch, and we had to drag him out of there. We walked over to the beach club and tried to explain to Caroline, but she lost her shit.

Did you not hear Mom when she said do not let him drive the Jeep under any circumstances?

I'd said, *A golf cart is not a car! Any fool can drive a golf cart!*

Everyone could hear us screaming in the parking lot, the Warner kids, making asses of themselves while their father sat on the club steps and ate clam chowder out of a paper cup.

Because that was what it was all about: soup. We all had Bloody Marys, and when Dad asked what the soup of the day was, Arturo said they had no soup. And that's when things went completely off the rails.

How could you not have soup? Did you run out? No? You just decided not to make any? Where's the manager? Where's Bobby? Bobby's not here? The assistant manager then, what's his name? Mark? Well, let me talk to Mark. Let me talk to Mark about making me, a dues-paying lifelong member of Sankaty, a cup of goddamned soup!

"Well," Caroline said as my father slurped the last drips of his soup. "You two better sit in the back with him. Sydney will ride up front with me."

"Oh, we can walk," I said.

"What?"

"We'll walk back to the club."

"Wait a minute—this isn't just about the soup, is it?" she said. "You came here to dump him on me? And you're going back to the fucking golf course?"

I blinked. My sister, the part-time crew coach, could have been a lawyer, a private investigator, the head of the fucking FBI. She was wasting her life when she could have been out berating people for a living.

"No, honey, not ex—" John started.

"What if he grabs the wheel, Tom? What if he unbuckles his seat belt and grabs the wheel and kills me and his granddaughter while you are fucking golfing?"

"Caroline, he is *not* going to do that."

"How do you know?"

"Fine, I'll go back with you."

"No, you will not."

"I won't?"

There was hope in my voice. That was another mistake I made. She heard it, of course, because my sister is a lioness who hears, smells, senses prey all around her.

"No," she said. "You are going to take him home. You. Alone. And my family will take the bus when we're done swimming."

"And what if he grabs *my* wheel, Caroline? That's okay?"

"Yes," she said between gritted teeth. "Because you have the least to lose."

Caroline

"Are we still going out for ice cream tonight?" Sydney asked as we rode the bus home.

"Yes," we said in unison.

"But first, we'll go to the store and get stuff for dinner after we drop Mommy off," John said.

Sydney was still young enough that going to the grocery store was interesting. Gum, PEZ, egg-shaped lip balms in every color. The magazines shimmered in their racks, promising all the adventures of adulthood. My daughter was still so sweet, but how much longer would we have before she turned into a terrifying adolescent? Four months? Five?

"What will you do, Mommy, while we're at the store?"

I turned and smiled at her, my golden girl. Her hair threaded with honey strands from the sun. The dusting of freckles across her nose that came back every summer and went away every winter, like an Etch A Sketch.

"I'll help Gran."

"What about Pop? Doesn't he need help too?"

I bit my lip, felt the swell of tears threatening behind my eyes. John glanced at me, and in that glance, we both knew: Sydney had noticed.

"Well, yes, honey, he does. He needs extra help now." I

explained that as people get older, they need more support and protection and patience.

"Does that mean grandparents aren't adults anymore?"

"What do you mean?"

"I mean, you have to listen to adults and do what they say. But if Pop tells me to do something, and I know it's not safe, I don't have to listen to him, right?"

"Honey," I said, my voice rising with alarm, "if anyone of any age tells you to do something and you know it's not safe, you shouldn't listen."

"You have to use your judgment," John said.

But was it that simple? My father could not be left alone. But could Sydney be left with him for even a minute? I already didn't like having my brother around her. He had always been selfish, unaware; he was clueless about protecting anyone. Not just his younger sister, when older boys were around. But a child? Forget it. He'd be focused on the television or his phone, turn his back when he should be watching. Sydney was a smart girl. Had she noticed? That I rarely left the room when the two of them were the only ones left in it? And how to explain that these people we purported to love, who we traveled with, who slept next to us in the rooms down the hall, were not to be trusted?

———

When we got home, my mother was on the porch, her clothes soaking, wringing out her hair.

"What?" she said. "I went for a dip."

I looked at her, then at John, and we had the exact same thought: Had both of my parents lost their minds at the exact same time?

Matt

Yes, I knew she was there, but that wasn't why I went over. I had information for Tom, and he was still my friend, practically the only one left who'd known me since grade school. People sometimes forgot that salient fact. I only saw him once a year, but we spoke frequently. I called him for wine advice; he called to ask about rentals or fishing for his clients who were visiting.

I waited until well past dinner—eight thirty—when I figured everyone would be calm and a bit liquored up. I heard them all—loud and raucous like a party with no music—almost as soon as I turned down Willard. Sound travelled a little too well in parts of Nantucket. Lack of trees, hills, vegetation to soak it up. Hulbert Avenue was a straight shot along the harbor, houses close together, no room for mature trees. You could hear it all: Rollerblades, mattress springs, laughter, babies crying, dogs barking. It was like being in the world's most expensive apartment building.

It was Caroline's voice I noticed first, low and strong, a little raspy. Sexy without her ever intending it to be. And terrifying when she was angry at you, and she was clearly angry at someone, though I only picked up the frequency, not the precise words.

As I parked and walked toward the porch, words were volleyed, and I heard scuffling, rustling, like someone was wrestling with a tree. Had to be the backyard. I ran to the gate, lifted the latch. Tom and another man I didn't recognize were struggling to hold on to Tripp Warner.

"Sorry to interrupt," I said. A ridiculous thing to say, but I had no idea what I'd walked in on.

"Matt," Tom said.

"Matt?" Caroline said.

"Matt, my boy!" Tripp bellowed.

"Hi, Warners," I said. "And…friends of Warners," I added, turning toward the man I didn't know.

"I'm John Stark," the stranger said.

"Caroline's better half?" I asked. I usually kept a low profile when she was there, not wanting to intrude. So I'd run into Caroline over the years, and her daughter, but somehow, never her husband. Or maybe I'd been avoiding him.

"On a good day," he said and smiled. It was not easy to smile while you were trying to keep a senior citizen in a grip lock.

"So where's Mrs. Warner?" I asked. Although I wanted to say "What's wrong?" or "Do you need handcuffs?"

"The Juice Bar," Caroline replied. "With Sydney."

"Sydney?"

"My daughter."

"Right. I knew that. Sorry for forgetting her name. I guess, you're…um, in the middle of something, but I needed to talk to Tom, and I heard you up the street—"

"We're lucky the police haven't arrived yet," Tom said ruefully.

"Well, you know how it is. Voices carry."

"Let go of me," Tripp Warner said. "So I can offer our esteemed guest a drink."

They finally relaxed their grip on him, but they didn't relax. No one in that house was the slightest bit relaxed.

"If this is a bad time—"

"What on earth makes you think this is a bad time, Matt?" Caroline said. "The screaming, the tussling, the fact that we're in the backyard with grass stains on our pants, tackling my father when he tried to climb the fence? Why, it's a perfect time to entertain."

I looked at her then, really allowed myself a look at her. The messy golden tips of her hair, making her appear carefree in a way I knew she wasn't anymore. Her solemn hazel eyes hardened as she locked them with mine. The wind picked up suddenly, and that could have explained the gooseflesh on my arms, but I know that wasn't it. It was because she was standing, squarely, in the same spot where their old tent had been. Did she feel it too? Every time she had to step back on that cold grass?

"I'll come back tomorrow," I said quietly.

"No," Tom said firmly. "I asked you to come, and you're not leaving."

"You *asked* him to come?" Caroline said.

"Yes," Tom replied. "Am I supposed to clear all my thoughts and behaviors with you, or can we just recognize that I am a separate adult human being and I have my own friends?"

"Now, now," Tripp said.

"You know what?" Caroline said. "I'm hungry for ice cream suddenly. I think I'll go see how Mom and Sydney are doing."

"There's pie in the kitchen," John said unhelpfully.

"Pie requires ice cream," she replied. "Everyone knows that."

She left, but not before casting a venomous glare at her brother. The wooden door banged behind her, a sound I heard all summer long.

"Let's go have some wine and pie, Matt," Tom said.

"Sounds excellent!" Tripp said.

"You've already had pie," Tom said.

"No, I haven't," Tripp replied.

And so we went to the front porch and ate blueberry pie and drank red wine. Red, white, and blue. This calmed him a bit, but overall, Tripp Warner was manic. That's the word I would use. He'd always been a lighthearted, fun person. A hugger, a slap-on-the-backer, the first to tell a joke. But now he was amped up, gritting his teeth every time he spoke.

John kept looking off in the direction of town, pacing at that end of the porch.

"The line was really long when I drove past," I said to him.

"Yeah," he said and looked at his watch. "My daughter's a slow eater," he added. "I'm just a little rattled by the whole beach assault thing."

"They probably won't come back via the beach."

"Right."

"The waffle cone takes a long time to eat," I said. "And maybe stopping to look at the boats decorated in the harbor."

"Yes, you're probably right," he said with a smile.

I liked Caroline's husband. Made me kind of sick to admit it, but I did.

We talked a little bit about fishing, where they were biting, what the tide situation was. Tripp seemed lost during this conversation. And John, well, John seemed to be standing guard in case Tripp decided to make a run for it. Tripp yawned finally, and Tom saw his opening.

"Dad," Tom said declaratively, "it's bedtime, don't you think?"

"What time is it?" Tripp asked, though he had a watch on his wrist.

"Midnight," Tom lied.

"Okay," Tripp said finally and stood up.

"You need any help, Dad?"

"Hell no."

John stood near the porch door for a few more minutes, listening. Teeth brushing, toilet flushing, the closing of the bedroom door. Finally, he came and joined us.

"You always said you wanted a second child," Tom said to John, who laughed, then checked his phone.

"Oh, they decided to stay and listen to the Cobbletones, an a cappella group. Apparently Sydney was taken with the lead singer."

I smiled. "Those guys are like the One Direction of Nantucket."

"Who's One Direction?" Tom asked.

"There's no hope for you," John said.

"So did you find anything out?" Tom said, clipping the end off his cigar.

"Yeah," I said and sighed. "I wish I had better news."

I explained that it was possible his neighbor was right—the widow's walk could be out of code after all. There was no permit filed, no plans I could dig up. I'd tracked down the guy who'd built it, a drunk named Old Bobby who told me he never did permits for little jobs. It wasn't worth the hassle and the cost, and no one ever checked back then. The historical society was after the bigger fish. I also mentioned I was pretty sure the homeowner was ultimately responsible for the permitting, not the contractor. Which didn't seem fair, and maybe could be fought in court—not that Tripp Warner was the litigious type. Not that it mattered. All that mattered now was getting the thing measured and surveyed.

"Do you think it's too high?" John asked.

Should I have told him the truth? That being up there had always felt wrong, not because it was someone else's house but because it seemed impossibly beautiful *and* impossibly high?

"Nothing is ever too high until it's in someone else's way," I said.

"That's a pretty Zen fucking answer," Tom said and laughed.

"It's true. And if he trespassed to get the information, well."

"Trespassed?"

I shrugged. "How else could he have determined how high it was unless someone measured?"

"I guess we should have installed surveillance cameras like some of our fancy new neighbors."

"Well," I said, "maybe some of your fancy neighbors have one of their cameras aimed at your house? Might show him trespassing."

"Huh," Tom said. "Could be useful."

"Something to think about," John said.

He stood and walked along the porch, eyes trained on the houses across the street. There were at least three cameras pointed this way. A few bike lights bobbed up the street from the left, and as the trio passed by, I saw that two of them were teenage girls still in their bathing suits, which seemed like madness. *Tourists*, I thought. Only tourists would leave home on an all-day bike ride without a sweatshirt.

Then, as they passed, a wolf whistle.

"What the fuck?" one of the girls said to the other.

"Nice rack!" a man yelled, and the girls slammed on their brakes and looked back at us.

"Pervert!"

Tom yelled back, "I'm sorry! It wasn't us!"

"The fuck it wasn't!" the other one called.

I exchanged a glance with John. I don't know which of us had the thought first, but he took off inside, and I followed, bounding up the two flights of stairs. The ladder to the widow's walk was already pulled down, and I could see the shadow of Tripp's legs standing above me.

"Jesus, Dad!" John said. "Get down here! You can't be doing this kind of shit!"

"I was sleepwalking!" Tripp replied.

"Well, were you sleep talking too? Acting like an old horndog to girls who are probably fifteen?"

"Oh, they had to be twenty," he said. "I just wanted to see everything."

"Okay, Dad. But you can't go up there alone, okay? It's not safe."

They settled him back in his room and closed the door. I went down to the kitchen, grabbed a couple of beer cans out of recycling and a length of kitchen twine from the pantry, and strung them together. I dangled them in front of Tom, told him to go hang them on Tripp's door.

"That should last for now, but you should consider a lock," I said.

"Not a bodyguard?" Tom sighed.

"Well, I think in handyman's terms," I said and shrugged.

As we walked out to the porch, Tom said he saw no reason to worry his sister with this little incident, and John nodded his head. He turned to me, eyebrows raised, as if I had some skin in the game, and I assured him I, of all people, sure as hell wasn't going to tell her.

Good God no, I would be the last one to tell Caroline Warner anything that could be used against me. I'd learned that lesson a long time ago.

FROM THE DESK OF LIEUTENANT
BILLY CLAYTON

Notes on Phone Interview with Tom Warner,
   Harassment Complaint, June 30, 2017
Admitted he was outside and saw the girls but
   claimed he didn't say anything to them
Indicated that he was aware of the recent beach
   assaults
Said tensions might be running high and people
   might be freaking out unnecessarily
Said there were no males in the house under the
   age of 45
Suggested we check the Brownstein property as
   sound travels on Nantucket

Alice

W hen my father purchased this house in the fifties, he got it for a song. I remember to this day how proud he was, telling my mother that he'd bought something set back from the beach, not on the beach. *All the views, none of the upkeep, and half the price.* Like he'd won. He'd strategized and made his move and was smarter than the rest of the ninnies who perched on the ocean. Of course, there were no homes blocking our view directly across the street from us then, just a small saltbox to the left and the right, catty-corner on either side.

He'd traveled alone to make the deal; my mother had approved on the basis of his description and his enthusiasm and her undying love for anything he did. My father was smart, and he made a wise deal for the time. He figured we'd summer here and his daughters would meet young men here and marry them here. And he was right. Sort of.

Tripp's family summered all the way on the eastern side, on 'Sconset, but to my parents, it may as well have been Mars. I still remember my mother explaining to a friend perusing real estate on the island: "'Sconset is somewhere you picnic, not somewhere you live."

To my parents, it was all about access. 'Sconset was too remote, the homes either too sprawling or too twee. Little sheds with roses. Almost like camping, I suppose, or glamping, as Caroline says they call it now. She tells me there's something called the tiny house movement, and so more and more people flock to 'Sconset every summer to see what is, most assuredly, the world's best example of it—I have never said 'Sconset and its rose-covered cottages and eastern beaches wasn't charming in its own way—but the idea of living out there, with all the erosion and the dreadful wind and all those tourists saying "Isn't it just darling?" was, and is, absurd. I remember my father asking Tripp if he slept on the porch of his cottage or in a hammock. And Tripp laughing heartily, assuring my parents that he slept in a proper bed, with a nightstand and a reading lamp and everything. He didn't tell them about the single bathroom and the outdoor showering, nor did he tell them about his summer job, working at 'Sconset Market, filling bushel baskets of food to be delivered to the North Bluff. He had a golf cart to buzz around in, or if the customers lived closer, at the larger cottages, sometimes he'd walk, the bushel half-balanced on his head like Carmen Miranda in a golf shirt.

Everyone's sons were expected to work to some degree; wealthy young men were admired for hard work and forays into entrepreneurship, even in the summer. But these were undertakings like Buzz Harrington's boat-cleaning business, or Skip Stewart bottling his mother's Bloody Mary mix. These were jobs that you made you think *What a go-getter.* I could just hear Mother wondering if Tripp could be taking his menial job from someone who needed it more. You had to leave things for others: the clothes at the thrift shop, the take it or leave it section of the dump, the jobs that an islander would be grateful for performing.

Of course, I was young, and I didn't think about such things. Tripp was happy, handsome, a good dancer; he was a good conversationalist, a good host who knew how to muddle mint and pour from a cocktail shaker. Those things seemed stylish and, therefore, important. That his happiness and conversation depended on the level of alcohol in his body had not occurred to me. I did not yet know that I could learn to see this, to gauge it like temperature or oil in a car. In the beginning, I suppose, it seemed like his tipsy self was his authentic self because he was drunk on love.

That his family was poor by Nantucket standards—not by anyone else's, mind you—concerned me not in the slightest. We met at the Independence Day Ball at the yacht club, each of us there with others, catching each other's eye on the dance floor. He said my hair was so pale and fine that the harbor lights were reflected off it, like I was wearing a headpiece of Christmas lights.

"Like an angel?" I said as I took a drag off his cigarette.

"No," he said, "more like St. Lucia, with a crown of lingonberry and candles."

"Lingonberry? Aren't you exotic."

"Well, you look Swedish. The feast of St. Lucia."

"Oh, I'm sure someone in my English family ran off with a Swedish nanny somewhere along the line. You're rather well-informed about the maiden traditions of other countries."

"History major," he said. And that should have been the end of it, I suppose, right there. Who didn't love history? Good God, we lived with it, the obsession with where we all came from, the pride of our past, the crests and trees and ancestors' stories whispered to children in the night. My mother loved to tell stories of our Mayflower ancestors, descended from John Smith. But Tripp was always silent about his family; he changed the topic, and of course, we knew his background was different. That his family had arrived later than mine, far later. Was that what spurred his college major, the obsession with why some people end up on the right side of history and some on the wrong?

I thought for a while, even after the children came along and the cocktail hour always seemed to run longer than an hour, that Tripp and I might still beat the odds. That we'd be one of "those couples," still annoyingly mad for each other, still pinching each other's rear end, still happy at the end of a long marriage. But that man is gone.

What on earth am I to do with him now? Send him out to golf and hope he doesn't jump off a cliff into the sea, while I rattle around this big house by myself and try to make new friends with all the awful people who've built up across the street, edge to edge, only a sliver of a walkway between them? Thank God for Beryl, Kip, Karen, still up the street, around the corner. Still holding strong against these others.

My father wanted a remove from the water, but oh, what a barrier these fools have created. They hug the cold sand, dug in, braced like a beach umbrella. So close to each other, they almost link arms to fight the breeze and rain and the clouds to keep them from going further. Keep it all, all the fury, all the danger, and yes, all the beauty.

When we sit on our porch, we see the lights in their kitchens, their garages, their fat brown packages from Restoration Hardware and L.L.Bean on their stoops. We watch their new Range Rovers coming and going, their security lights blinking on and off every time a rabbit skitters near. The same way we used to watch the lighthouse, the ferry, the red dinghies bobbing in the blue waves.

Now, instead of wide swaths of a view, there is only an inch of ocean-y blue between houses, a blue that pulses now, bolder and more vibrant than I remember it, fighting to be seen.

And the assault now coming from all sides! That awful man behind us thinking his view is more important than ours, because he has more property, more house, more toys, more gall than anyone I've ever met!

Back in my parents' time, when someone bought a piece of land or, God forbid, renovated—a word we barely knew back then, for who did such things? Who tore apart the core of a house, ripping out its soul, in an attempt to make it better? Is there anything sadder than an oven yanked from a wall, a washer and dryer pulled from a closet, silvery hoses flailing about behind them like space men lost, untethered?—yes, back then when anyone dared to take a project on, we had them over for drinks on the porch, to remind them of our sight lines, to subtly ask them to be sensitive to this view that we all share. And they were. Of course they were!

We all knew each other. We were from different states, yes, and different country clubs, but all of us, up and down the street, were in the Social Register. That was reassuring. There was a time when all of Nantucket was like that in the summer, and that's part of what people hate about it, but it's what I loved about it, always, that sameness. And I don't think that's wrong. We clammed together; we fished together; our children ran in a tanned and towheaded tribe up and down the beach. We did the same things, yes, but more importantly, *we believed in the same things.* Or thought we did.

We believed in fresh air and cold, bracing water. We believed in cocktail hour and afternoon tea. We had chairs on our front porches, but we believed in motion, in not sitting still. We believed in growing things, tending things, keeping them up instead of trying always to keep up. We boarded our children in school, but not our dogs. We named our boats, but never our houses. We didn't believe that bigger and newer was better. Quite the contrary. Older and smaller made us feel best. Cozy and worn down a bit, broken in. The smell of new things felt wrong, plastic, horrifying. Where was the fresh air? Where was the sun bleaching everything fresh? *What is this new obsession with new?*

This way of life fell out of favor, and people think it's coming back now, with all the organic farming and recycling and so forth. But it's not the same. Those people, the farm-to-tablers, and the back-to-nature minimalists I keep reading about—they aren't like we were. They care so much, think so fervently, too much about everything. We didn't care; we just believed, and we did. We cared so little! Our insouciance about it all—holes in our clothing, scrapes on our knees—so what? I look at Caroline's friends, who research everything and think through every little decision, and I think, *Wasn't life so much easier when we didn't give a rat's behind, when we didn't have to know so much?*

How things have changed! People don't wish to know one

another. No one cares if they do business with a stranger. Uber, Craigslist, all those things—it's madness. That's part of what's happened in Nantucket, what's gone on across the street. The problem isn't renovating so much as it is selling. Once a house leaves a family, once they sell to a stranger, to someone with no history and no understanding of the way things used to be done, well, that was the end. The new people have no interest in the old ways. The proper, decent ways. No. They are selfish; they turn away.

They orient themselves toward the harbor, the vastness of the sea, toward what is out there, not what is in here. Not toward us. They don't have to look at us, but we have to look at them. And they prefer it that way.

And yes, sometimes, I confess, I sit on the porch watching the clouds gather, the squall forming, the inevitable nor'easters that come in the fall, and I wish it on them. For that is how I have come to think of it: them, and us. Let their slate crack. Let the wind lift all their hand-carved shutters. Let the waves rush into their basements, with their pool tables and their viewing rooms, and let their flat-screen TVs be taken out to sea! I'll sit here, on the rise above them, and let them take the hit for me, over and over and over again. And that man who lives behind us, that awful, awful man, he was just biding his time, I knew. Just staking his claim until he could leap over my house and go to live on the other side. Well, I would see about that.

After I'd come home and toweled off, I put on my thinking cap. And I got out my trusty old camera.

Tom

It wasn't easy to sleep late in Nantucket. Our window shades were cheap—pale and thin and generally no match for the orange sunrise. The rooms that faced east, like mine, fairly glowed from 5:00 a.m. on a clear day. Then there were the birds, with their array of voices. If the songbirds signaling each other didn't wake you up, the seagulls cracking oyster shells would finish the job. Arriving next, around 7:00 a.m., were the gardeners, with the whine of their weed whackers and hedge clippers. And then, a little before eight, the construction workers with their nail guns and saws. Whoever petitioned the courts to outlaw waterskiing and small watercraft in the harbor needn't have bothered; the most annoying things on Nantucket were on land, not on the sea.

The morning after my father's little escapade, however, I woke up to the rhythm of a basketball on pavement, followed by the squeak of backboard.

I woke up, rubbed my eyes, looked out the window. Where was this fresh hell coming from? I put on my shorts and a shirt and walked downstairs, out to the porch, where my mother and sister sat, not talking to each other, reading different sections of the *Globe*, pausing to sip their tea.

No one ever sat inside when they could sit outside. No one ever showered inside when they could shower outside. No one swam in a pool when they could swim in an ocean. No one drove a car when they could take a bike. There were no hammocks or chaises or ottomans. Only rockers, the chair that encouraged you to move. The mattresses were thin and unyielding. The toilet seats were unsteady and cracked. Everything about this house said *Don't get too comfortable.*

So most of the time, on the porch, drinking a hot beverage, that was the only relaxing moment of the day.

"Good morning," I said, my voice still froggy.

"There's a quiche in the oven," my mother replied.

"Then it's an even better morning. What kind?"

"Bacon and tomato and—"

"I caramelized the onions," Caroline said.

"I'll engrave that on your trophy," I said and sighed.

"The onions take longest," my mother said, patting her hand. "They're the hardest part."

"Waiting is the hardest part," I said. "When it smells so amazing."

"Flattery will get you a second slice."

"I hope so. Where's the rest of the crew?"

My mother's lips were set in a tight pair of lines I was all too familiar with. They were the only thing that stood between her propriety and her fury. Two thin lines.

"Well, your father broke into the Groves' yard through a double-latched gate to help himself to their new basketball hoop, and your sister allowed her daughter to be his accomplice."

"Wow. Heading to juvie already. Very impressive."

"Maybe she takes after her uncle," Caroline said.

"It's not funny, you two," my mother said. "It's trespassing, and I don't approve."

"Mom, you've known the Groves for years."

"That only makes it worse, Tom, and you know it."

"Mom," Caroline said, "honestly, with kids these days, I think we have to pick our battles."

"Is that right?" she said with a sniff.

"There should be more yeses than nos."

"What about battling with our neighbors? Don't we have enough strife on that front?"

My father walked up the street, calling out, "Anyone up for a mountain bike ride?" His hair was sweaty, his face red, his smile wide.

"How about a walk on the beach," my mom suggested.

"Or a jog!" my father said. "Sydney and I can race!"

"How about breakfast?" I said.

"Let's go to the beach first!" my father cried.

There was no rest in these people. I was the only person named Warner who ever got tired. Caroline and Dad bounced their legs the same way when they sat; did they even know that? And my mother, well, she never sat unless she was peeling a potato or writing a letter.

"Fine," I said. It was a beautiful day, and a walk on the beach was innocuous enough for Dad and alcohol-free for me and John. I think Caroline would carry a breathalyzer in her pocket if she could.

We crossed the street like a set of ducklings, in a row by height, John and I holding up the back, making sure Dad didn't take a detour. Dad looked at everything differently now—every neighbor's arched gate a portal, every Frisbee an invitation, each red plastic shovel on the beach an instrument of buried treasure.

My father was a child. Not the drooling aged infant we all fear, but a playful ten-year-old, when the joy of movement rang in your limbs, before adolescence hijacked your every thought. All the things Caroline accused me of—of perpetual college, of permanent boyhood, of Peter Panning—I saw now in my dad. And how much happier, how much more settled, would my sister be if she could do the same thing? Skip back to that time, before the whole world conspired against her to fuck her up permanently?

Caroline, Sydney, and John hunted for sea glass, my mother picked up trash, and Dad and I would have started skipping rocks if there had been more flat ones, but there weren't.

"We should have a clambake," my father said. "On July 4."

"Yes, we should."

"Remember the ones we used to have?"

"Yes." I smiled. Dad would invite the whole neighborhood, and everyone would bring whatever they'd caught or dug up that day. Clams, mussels, striper. Bluefish if there wasn't enough striped bass. We provided chowder, bread, and gin and tonics. I'd been taught how to make one at the age of nine. It was what Dad's parents had done in 'Sconset, and he started the tradition in his new home on Hulbert Avenue.

My father didn't know how to use a blender, boil an egg, or run the dishwasher, but he knew how to catch and clean any kind of fish. Not just from the boat, searching for the edge of the shoal, finding the hidden pockets, but also later, at dusk, straight off the beach. He taught every one of my friends how to use a fishing rod; even random kids on the beach could get a casting lesson. He always brought an extra couple of rods, and soon, there would be a line of us, hauling them in. He'd run to each of us, helping, enjoying the look on our faces when we caught a keeper. There was a physical satisfaction to it, like throwing a perfect spiral or hitting a line drive.

After we ate, we would sit around the bonfire until it died down, and Dad took all the kids out for ice cream. Not at the Juice Bar, because that was for tourists. We went all the way out to 'Sconset Market, and my father doled out the cones to all the kids, advising them on flavors, ruffling their hair, and pretending to take bites. Other kids loved my dad, which had only served to make my sister angry. She didn't want to share him. He loved everybody, and that made her believe he loved her less.

"We never ran out of chowder," he said, smiling. "Your mother always had more, no matter how many people came."

"I never thought of that before."

"Sometimes there were hundreds of people!"

"Dad, I don't think so—"

"Yes! Lined up all up and down Jetties Beach on towels!"

"Okay," I said.

"She could have sold it. I'd be a wealthy man."

"You are a wealthy man, Dad," I said, and he reached over and squeezed my hand, as if to say I was one of his riches.

My mother never told anyone what exactly she put in the chowder; she claimed to have a top-secret ingredient. Caroline had received the recipe on her wedding day, in a silver recipe box, and had told me the following summer: rum. Dark rum and Worcestershire sauce.

My dad and I waded ankle deep.

Sydney ran up to us, her sweatshirt gathered around her haul.

"Look at all I found!" she said.

"Hell's bells," my father cried. "It's like sunken treasure!"

She held up shards of almost every color—brown, green, even aqua. I thought of all the parties it took to produce this much glass. How long it took to soften the edges of broken beer bottles, wine, whiskey. I liked thinking that some of these bottles, some of these eroded memories, were from me. I fingered the edge of a larger piece of brown glass; it was still sharp on one end, too new. Probably a damned IPA.

"That one's probably too sharp," she said. "I should put it in recycling."

"Or you could keep it in your pocket as a weapon. To fight off monsters."

"You've been talking to my mom," she said.

"Au contraire. Your mom has been talking to me."

She slipped the glass into the pocket of her jean shorts and smiled. I smiled back at her.

My dad turned suddenly and yelled back to my mom. "Alice," he yelled. "Why the hell don't you make chowder for us anymore? I miss that chowder!"

"Dad," I said quietly, touching his arm, "we had it last night. And you had it for lunch."

When we walked home, my father looked over at the Groves' house hopefully. "Hey, guys," he said. "How about another b-ball game?"

"No," my mother said.

"Mom," I said, "the Groves won't care if Dad and Sydney use their hoop. They're not even here."

"How do you know?" Caroline asked.

How did I know? How to explain that one of the things I did every year was take inventory—of which house was occupied and which was not, scanning the neighborhood automatically, looking for lights on, blinds up, garage doors open or closed. It was a holdover from my youth when I needed vacant houses to smoke pot, drink, have sex with girls I met on the strip. Had the statute of limitations run out on confessing this?

"I did not ask you to come here early to gang up on me," my mother hissed. "In case my intentions weren't clear."

"Mom, we're not ganging up on you."

"The hell you aren't. I need your support, not your...your... conspiracy."

Caroline's face flushed red, as it often did when she was mad. She hated that visible evidence, always had. She'd run and hide when she felt herself blushing. She had never wanted anyone to know her. She wanted them to serve her, not know her. That's what I told Matt Whitaker when they broke up. Matt carried a torch right up to her wedding, and then his. And coming over to our house every week, hammering and nailing, patching it up in all the broken places. I wanted to take him by the shoulders and tell him to give it up. *You can't fix her.*

Now, John was Caroline's indentured servant. I liked the guy plenty—he was a great guy. He was exactly who I'd pick to be my indentured servant too.

"He's breaking the law."

"Oh, come on, Mom. What's the worst that can happen?" I said.

"He could be captured on camera and arrested for trespassing!"

"The Groves don't have surveillance cameras trained on their basketball hoop."

"Well, perhaps they asked someone like a neighbor to keep an eye out, and that person photographed the evidence and submitted it to the police! Then what?"

"What?"

"Well, you never know what your neighbors might be documenting, that's all I'm saying. I mean, with a pervert on the loose, we can't be too vigilant, can we? We should all keep our eyes open wide."

I exchanged another glance with my sister. It was all I could do to not make the "cuckoo" motion with my finger and head.

"Mom," I said with a sigh, "you have a very active imagination."

"No," she said sternly. "I have very sharp eyesight."

**FROM THE DESK OF LIEUTENANT
BILLY CLAYTON**

Notes on Arrest of Bear Brownstein, Indecent
    Exposure, July 1, 2017

Suspect accused of exposing himself on his
    property, specifically, urinating into bushes

Surrendered without protest when approached at
    home with warrant

Kept asking about evidence (photo exhibit 1)

Blamed his plumber for shutting off water, then his
    neighbor for following him and taking photos

Posted bail within an hour

Alice

Yes, I took the pictures. It was like bird-watching—nothing more, nothing less. An animal will always reveal himself inside his natural habitat, won't he? Cutting through the neighbors' yards repeatedly after a walk or swim. And then, the pièce de résistance: relieving himself in his own bushes one day.

And calling the head of the Sankaty new membership committee, to tell them that one of their proposed new members was the focus of a criminal investigation, and perhaps they should be moved back to the bottom of the waiting list until this was sorted out?

Well, that was just good, solid committee work. Performed by the outgoing secretary of said committee and very much appreciated by the new members of that committee. Because it was one thing to be a Jew; it was quite another to be a pervert.

What can I say? Some birds don't know the landscape as well as they should. They build their nests in the wrong place.

The next morning, though, I made a few small mistakes. Like forgetting John had a habit of waking early. Like leaving the scissors and newspaper scattered over the kitchen table when I went outside. The room even smelled of newspaper, the blue tang of ink, but dry and tindery, like the moment before you light a fire. Not that John would notice that; Caroline would, not him.

The pile looked midproject; he would probably think Sydney had made the mess. So I thought afterward. But when I walked in from the porch, my feet still damp, and ran smack into him, well, he startled me. I flushed. I know I did.

"Good morning," he said.

"Good morning, John. I was just...taking out the...recycling."

He blinked. We both knew the recycling was kept inside, then loaded into the Jeep to be driven to the dump. We didn't have garbage pickup. No one in the house took out the recycling to anywhere but the car.

"Oh," he said.

"I guess Sydney can clean her art project mess when she's up," I said. "Or I'll just do it now."

I went outside toward the garbage cans, put away the scraps in a bucket, used the small tap under the house to wash my hands. When I came back to the stairs, John was drinking coffee on the back porch, looking across the Brownsteins' property, fingering a pair of binoculars around his neck.

I swallowed hard. At the back of the Brownsteins' property, on the small lot they'd taken over, the one with the cottage Caroline had always called a hidey-hole for its ivy-colored, hobbit-like cuteness, there was only a giant maw now, gray with concrete. Was there anything uglier than a house under construction?

And now, beside the gaping hole, a new, bright-green Porta-Potty. This addition made me smile—no more public urinating for Mr. Brownstein or his workers! I'd taken care of that!

The wind picked up suddenly, and I heard the paper flapping just as I saw John lift the binoculars to his eyes.

Surely, John couldn't see it. But even if he did, would he connect it to the newspaper scraps?

I really needed to be more careful in covering my tracks next time.

Maggie Sue

He was usually gone when I arrived; where he went off to, who knows. Golf, maybe, not fishing or tennis. No rod holders on his car. No white shorts in his closet. He walked on Jetties Beach sometimes—I'd seen him once or twice, cutting across the spit on his way home—but he didn't look seaworthy. Walked a little unsteady, to tell the truth, listed side to side like a bird. Like a creature used to not walking. Hard to imagine him balancing on a prow, reeling in a fish. Or taking any kind of chances, for that matter. One time, he was on his way out, and he stopped and asked me to get him a book high on a shelf. Said he got vertigo on the library ladder, and did I mind? He'd laughed when I asked him if he kept his favorite books on the bottom shelves.

I was early that day when I found the poster, seven forty-five instead of eight, because there was no line at the Fog Island takeout window. I ate my egg biscuit in the car, left the wrapper there. Didn't feel right throwing my trash in with his.

The porch was still dewy in places, a few stray leaves fluttering around. I'm not paid to clean the exterior, but I always sweep the porch when I finish, because what good is a clean house with a dirty porch?

I pushed in the alarm code, took off my shoes, left them in

the foyer. I usually clean top to bottom unless someone gives me a good reason not to, but first, I check the kitchen to see if there's a note. Nobody ever leaves you a note anywhere but the kitchen.

Not sure what made me look outside. The ongoing construction was nothing special to me—especially before July 4. Crews work overtime, and trucks and backhoes beep their warnings constantly, more annoying than crows at daybreak, but you get used to it. The nail guns, the saws, it all stops around 4:00 p.m., and then *poof*, you can hear the water and seagulls again. But the workers were gone that day.

More likely, it was the bright wildflowers, the meadowy backyard, the wild roses still going strong. I opened the kitchen window to catch a whiff, because the smell of real roses never gets old, especially after a day spent with people's fake candles and scented cleansers and whatnot. Through the open window, I saw something. Something flapping and torn.

The exterior is not my domain—I won't wash down anyone's porch furniture unless there's a gun put to my head. But I have an eye for what's wrong or right. When something is out of place or doesn't belong.

And that's what made me open the door and walk outside with my yellow rubber gloves on, through the lush backyard. The old cottage was gone, the footings for the pool house were poured, the framing about to start. The offshore wind was whipping that day; I'd seen all the windsurfers and kiteboarders in the harbor as I drove by, dancing up and down like bright toys in a bathtub. Now a poster was blowing in that same wind, taped at the top of the Porta-Potty, half-ripped from its mooring. I reached up with one gloved hand and peeled it off the rest of the way. I carried it in the house, smoothed it out on the table.

And then I called him, right away, so he could think through his options. And also, I admit, so he wouldn't for one second think that I would put up something that said *Jews are not wanted here* on his property.

FROM THE DESK OF LIEUTENANT
BILLY CLAYTON

Investigation of Trespassing, Brownstein Property,
July 2, 2017

Poster with derogatory message taped to structure
on his property (photo 1)

No security cameras

No destruction to property or person

Claims the Warners "had it in for him," that this
is the second "hate crime" perpetrated against
him

No witnesses, no positive ID

Became belligerent when I had to leave to investigate Warner incident at Surfside (does not
appear to be connected)

Tom

I
t was Mom's idea to go out to the beach together, I think
now because she wanted to get away, to hide. We argued a
bit about which beach to go to—Dad wanted to go where the
highest waves were, and Caroline wanted her daughter to have a
lifeguard, a bathroom, a snack bar. So we settled on Surfside. We
packed a cooler, and of course, I put some wine in it. It's called
vacation, people! I chose bottles I thought were lighter, appropriate
for lunch. I chose what my sister might actually like, not that she'd
ever give me credit for it. A rosé, a Sancerre.

We had just walked down the steps, smoothed the blankets,
unfurled the umbrellas, opened the portable table, and as I handed
my sister a glass of wine, describing why I liked this particular rosé,
Caroline interrupted.

"Please," she said. "It's all bullshit. Blackberry this, mango that.
Contains hints of mischief and notes of ransom."

"Well, all sales are a bit of a rogue's business, aren't they?" my
mother said.

"Are you actually telling me that you can't taste any flavors
when you drink this?"

"I taste grapes," Caroline said.

"Last night, I picked up on the tobacco in that zinfandel," John
said. "Just like you said."

At moments like this, I am sure that there is a God and that he sent John to our family for me, not just for my sister.

"It's bullshit," she repeated.

"You, who grips the Zagat guide when you pick a restaurant? Are you saying food critics are liars as well?"

"Food can be proven," Caroline replied.

"What the hell does that mean?"

"I mean, in the lab. The science of it. Like on *America's Test Kitchen.*"

"There's plenty of science in wine, Caroline, good God. You can prove that there are elements in common with the fruit—"

"You sell unopened bottles you find in a crazy person's cellar. How can you tell how old it is or what it tastes like?"

I shook my head. "Do you really want to know?"

"Yes, yes, of course we would," Mom said.

"Wine can be authenticated, much the way a museum can look at an artifact—"

"By the age of the bottle," Mom added.

"Sometimes. But glass can be tricky to pinpoint. Sometimes you can tell by the etching techniques, or the type of drill used, if there are initials etched on it. And then there's the radioactivity."

"Radioactivity?" John said.

"Yes. Bottles from after 1960 emit lots more radiation, because of the above-ground nuclear testing."

"You're making that up," Caroline said.

"I wish I was."

"I'm never drinking wine again," John said.

"Until tonight," Dad added, and we all laughed.

We finished lunch, I finished the wine, and when Sydney said she wanted ice cream, Dad said he did too. We were only twenty feet from the ramp leading up the dune to the snack bar. But my sister watched the two of them carefully. So carefully. Up, up the wooden ramp. So close by, but still she watched. I saw her fingering the phone in her hand, as if she saw it coming. As if the intent, the desire to call 911 was in her limbs already.

As soon as Sydney and Dad were out of sight above the dune, she stood up. She saw something. She knew something. Then she ran. Before the rest of us even had a second to worry, she ran. The sand kicking off her heels, fine as dust, like the aftershock of an explosion. We stood then—Mom, me, and John, running after her, but all unsure. We didn't know, but Caroline did.

Her lack of trust, her rocketing fury, maybe that's what set it in motion. Dad must have seen the missile of her anger coming toward him, gathering speed. And he did the only natural thing, the only thing he could do. He capitalized on his head start. He grabbed Sydney's hand and ran. Caroline had imagined he'd do something heinous, and so he did. You don't want to disappoint Caroline.

The keys were in the surf van; of course they were. The couple who ran the business were just a few feet away, talking to customers, arranging payment, sizing up ability, charming beginners, pointing to the small waves. We arrived just as Dad swung the van into reverse. The boards strapped to the top wobbled; inside, the wet suits swung wildly on their plastic hangers. Sydney squealed as loudly as the tires, knowing she was doing something wrong, and knowing, also, that it was fun. Fun as fucking hell.

"I think I know where he's headed," I said, panting.

"He told you? He told you and you—"

"No. Jesus Christ, Caroline! I just know how his mind works."

"Tell us your theory, Tom," my mother said.

"He's taking her for ice cream," I said. "Like he used to with us—to 'Sconset Market, or—"

"How do you know that?"

"What else makes any sense? The line was long, so he went somewhere else."

"You," Caroline said. She jabbed her long, tanned finger in my face, all straight lines, no smooth places left. "You think that makes sense? Stealing a van with a child to avoid a line?"

"To him it does."

"But earlier—he wanted to go to the South Shore, where the waves were higher. Maybe he went there?" John added.

Caroline took a deep breath and looked away. I imagine she had to do that all the time to diffuse the time bomb of her perpetual anger. She called 911, covering her other ear with her hand, drowning out the crowd, the surf.

We waited five or ten minutes. My mother refolded our towels, stacked them on top of the basket.

"We should head home," Mom said.

"I'm not going home while my child is missing!"

"She's not missing, Caroline. She's with her grandfather!"

"Who kidnapped her!"

"Oh dear God, Caroline, he didn't kidnap her! I hope to God you don't say that to the police!"

"I didn't have to! That is an accurate description of the situation, Mother! He carjacked the van and kidnapped a child!"

John looked at his feet, as if wishing they could carry him away. Is there anything sadder than a good man married to an angry woman?

"Mother," she said evenly. "This is what you were afraid of. What you knew he was capable of! What did you witness before you came up here?"

"Witness?"

"What did he do before that you didn't tell us, Mother?"

Mom turned away, her lips set in a straight line. *Christ*, I thought. *Caroline is right. Something happened.*

John put his arm gently around his wife, barely touching her, reeling her in. He whispered in her ear, and she shook her head, violently. We stood there for a few more minutes before the young officer arrived, started taking notes, and the call came in through the police radio.

He turned to us and said they'd been found, taken into custody.

"Where?" I asked suddenly, because it suddenly mattered. It would fall to me and John.

"He was heading to Altar Rock," he said.

The highest point of land on the island.

FROM THE DESK OF LIEUTENANT
BILLY CLAYTON

Investigation of Stolen Van, Surfside, July 2, 2017

Van pulled over after turning onto Altar Rock Road

Tripp Warner driving, Sydney Stark passenger

Mr. Warner said he was just borrowing the van to
    "get away from all the naysayers"

Surf Adventure owners agreed to not pursue
    charges when Mr. Warner offered to buy a
    surfboard and wet suit

Alice

We coaxed Tripp into the wicker love seat on the porch, far from the door and the stairs. Propped up his feet, settled a pillow beneath his head. Tom took the damned surfboard and wet suit down to the basement to hide them. I would have preferred sending them straight to the dump.

I stood there for a long time watching over Tripp, as if he was a baby. His skin nearly as soft and plump as a child's too. So unfair that he should be this unlined, unmarked by life. Hadn't we experienced all the same things? Had I simply felt them all more deeply, and they'd carved themselves into my face like a painful tattoo? His hair only dusted with gray, mine overcome with it. His eyelashes still long. Sometimes when I look back on our photos, I almost look like his mother. Or older sister, at least. Is this why, I wonder—so I'd love him even now when he was broken in two, so clearly not himself? Only when he stripped off his clothes, layer by layer, could you truly see where gravity had reached him, where flesh hung off bone, where skin had given up, let itself down, down, down, in relief. I look like that too, everywhere. My breasts are deflated and, at the same time, relaxed, no longer tired of all the trying and posing. The body at rest, finally. That's what I see at dusk down by the water, when I bike over to that sliver of public way next to the Galley some of the locals call the

Gaza Strip. The ladies unabashed in their flowered suits and bathing caps, their husbands nowhere in sight. It's the same thing I see at art museums, the Botticellian happiness of not trying to be anything you are not. Relief. Joy. Gravity.

"We have to watch him more carefully," I whispered through the screen door to Tom and John. They sat next to each other, checking their phones, silent as toddlers playing with their own trucks. They stood up, walked out to the porch, as if I needed them then, at that instant.

"You mean *we* have to watch him," Tom said.

"We'll work in shifts."

"Alice," John said softly, "he probably needs to go into a facility."

"I am all too aware of that," I said and sighed.

"Maybe I can help with the research?"

"Yes, John, that would be lovely."

"Or Caroline probably knows some places," he added.

"Does she now? Has she been planning for our demise?"

"You shoulda quit while you were ahead, John," Tom said.

"I just mean she knows a lot of people who've gone through similar things. With parents and…grandparents, et cetera."

Tom and I exchanged looks. He had the same skin as his father, plump and golden, the German in them, I supposed. Almost buttery looking, delectable, as he was as a child. Caroline more thin skinned, stretched, brittle. Was that all it was? The only difference, destiny in skin?

Sydney came out to the porch and whispered, "Is Grandpop asleep?"

"Yes," John said. "Are you feeling tired too?"

"Nope."

"All the excitement didn't wear you out?" Tom asked, looking up from his phone.

"It wasn't that exciting, because we never got to that exciting place he was talking about," she said and sighed. "Guess he didn't drive fast enough."

"So he…drove slowly?" I said, relieved that he'd done something, finally, right.

"Yeah. People were honking at us because he couldn't find the turn."

John looped an arm around her shoulder. "Well, we were worried because that, um, that van didn't belong to Pop, you know?"

"When he told me to get in, he said he was borrowing it. And that we'd be right back. And that it was okay with Mom."

Everyone nodded. It made perfect sense, and I was relieved that they weren't going to blame the child for doing something that seemed natural—going for a drive with her grandfather.

"Well, always check with us first," John said.

Caroline had disappeared, as she sometimes does, nowhere to be found. Soaking in a bath, taking a power walk, I didn't know. I just knew she was prone to this, to not being around when she was needed. Letting John take up the slack. So worried about her father and her daughter, and yet she would leave them both and go off to do whatever.

Oh, the thought of me doing that when Tripp and I were younger! When I think of all that could have gone wrong or gone undone. I used to tell my girlfriends that Tripp couldn't make a sandwich without me in the house. Didn't know where the knives were, the toppings, the bread. The questions I fielded from upstairs: *Where are the napkins? Where is the milk?* Tom and Caroline innocently asking him for something while I bathed, and him keeping it a secret that he did not know how to fill their simple, earnest needs. He'd make a joke, tickle them, suggest a game, anything to kill time before their mother came downstairs and could do whatever needed to be done. But I didn't care, no, that's the truth of it, because I was particular. I preferred things done a certain way, and he would never be able to perform them up to snuff. My friends joked about "training" their husbands, but mine would have required boot camp.

My children learned how to work, to be independent, though

there is nothing like adolescence to make you throw up your hands and stop trying. The only way to deal with it, really. I see Caroline now with Sydney, though, doing the opposite. Hanging in there, on the sidelines, as if she can still change the outcome. And I want to shout, to scream from the rooftops, *It won't work. Don't waste your breath! Just let her go, and when she's twenty-one, she'll find her own way home if you leave out snacks and vodka for her friends!*

But no, Caroline is always hovering, always suggesting. *Why don't you. How about you.* Go here, go there, take this, make that. Ninety-nine percent of what she says is dismissed, of course, because who wants to hear suggestions all the time. Who wants a drone in their ear? And then she starts in on me, suggesting activities for Sydney and me to do together. *To create memories,* which is a phrase I'd like to banish from the dictionary forever. I don't want to *go catch* hermit crabs. I want to exclaim over them when she brings them to me! She needs playmates, and she needs a family, each distinct from the other.

When Tom and Caroline were young, they only came home when they were hungry or bleeding. They swam; they took out the dinghy in the harbor; they rode their bikes to the yacht club to play ping-pong or find a tennis match. And yes, they sometimes found more adventure than they bargained for. A dead body, tangled in the spartina down at Jetties after a storm. Broken beer glass on the beach when they were running barefoot. These things happen.

Caroline was so strong and brave as a child, she was almost like a boy—because I made her that way. There was no makeup on a vanity for her to play with, no hairspray, no perfume, nothing but Chap Stick. We gave her sports equipment, lessons, not dresses. But now she's turned into a nervous Nellie, a veritable handwringer around her daughter. Once I was visiting and had to pick Sydney up at dance class when her mother ran late—and Caroline gave me their secret code word! Can you imagine? *Koala.* As if that could keep her safe. As if she should be taught that one should be wary of grandparents too! *Why don't you just lock her up until she's eighteen?* I'd said. And Caro had looked at me with those hazel eyes that could turn almost yellow when she was angry and informed me that the world is a dangerous place. Well, of course it can be! I'm not an idiot. But it's as if she doesn't realize it's the exposure to things—the nicks and bruises—that form you, that make you strong and certain.

Would she have ever married a gentle man like John if she hadn't encountered a couple of rough young men in her own backyard?

"Could we fly off-island and get him seen in Boston?" Tom asked.

"Getting him seen isn't the issue, Tom. He's been seen."

"Well, maybe he needs more tests. Maybe they missed something?"

"Caroline and I wondered if he was having a reaction to medication," John said.

"He's not on any medication," I said and sighed. "And he has a doctor appointment scheduled when we get back."

"I guess you can't hire a bodyguard on Nantucket," Tom replied.

"Oh, you probably can get one on the Cape," John said and smiled.

Tom laughed. It was something Tripp always said, that you could get it on the Cape, as if that was easy. As if that was close or convenient when you're a two-hour ferry ride away.

"But he needs a kind of hybrid. A nurse-slash-commando."

"He'll have to make do with you two," I said. "One of you can be the nurse and the other commando."

"I call commando," Tom said. That was the world, wasn't it? No one wanted to be a nurse to anyone anymore, and that was that. Not even me. Especially me.

"So we let him sleep, then what?"

"Then do something that isn't criminal," Tom said.

"And that isn't surfing," Sydney added, and we all laughed.

Caroline

When I returned from my walk, I saw an envelope stuck in the screen door. *Great*, I thought. Another missive from our neighbor? Maybe he'd like us to remove our porch as well as our widow's walk. But as I got closer, coming up the porch stairs, I saw the shaky handwriting and old-fashioned cursive spelling out *Tripp & Alice* that signaled it was from a senior citizen.

"Hopefully a happier piece of mail," I said, dropping it in my mother's lap.

I drank a glass of water and put the kettle on for tea. She opened the letter, sighed, then got up and threw it in the trash.

"What was that?"

"An invitation to cocktails tonight."

"From someone you don't like?"

"No, from Beryl."

I frowned. Beryl was one of my mother's closest friends. "Are you mad at her or something?"

"Of course not."

"Then why—"

"Caroline," she said and sighed. "I don't want our friends to see your father like this."

"Mom, Dad loves parties. And his friends would understand."

"No, it's…undignified. God knows he can't go back to Sankaty after his stink about the soup."

"What are we going to do, keep him locked inside? He'll want to go places. We'll run into people he knows."

"I know," she said.

"Maybe they could help him? His friends might have… suggestions."

"Dear God, Caroline," she said. "I don't want to put him on display if I don't have to. He already RSVP'd to something on the fifth, so I don't quite know what we'll do about that."

"Well, maybe he'll be better by then," I said.

My mother smiled and nodded at me, but there was pity in her eyes. The same look she'd given my dad when he'd insisted on stopping and smelling the roses.

I went and sat on the porch as my mother banged around in the kitchen, waiting for Dad to wake up, swapping ideas for what the hell we could do with him.

"He seems to gravitate toward adventure," John said, and I shot him a look. "Just trying to lighten things up," he said, sighing.

"Maybe we could take him out on the boat?" Tom said.

"Jesus, Tom. What if he decided to swim to the Vineyard?" I said.

"He wouldn't do that."

"Yesterday, he wouldn't hijack a van either."

"If we take him to Children's Beach, I guess he'd be suspicious."

"No, we could stay near the pier. Say we're going to see the boats—lure him by saying we're getting a drink afterward at the White Elephant."

"A drink somewhere other than the club?" Tom said in mock horror. "That you'd have to pay cash for? What was it Dad always used to say about carrying money?"

"*Only poor men own wallets*," I said.

"Ouch," John said.

"He also said *Only Jews carry change*."

"Double ouch."

"I hope the next time I fall asleep, no one stands over me remembering my worst attributes," Tom said and sighed.

"You started it," I replied.

John clapped his hands. "So, boats? Children's Beach? Drink at the White Elephant?"

"Only if it's one drink," I said. "One."

I went upstairs, brushed my hair, and brushed my teeth. Something about brushing my teeth midday made me feel better, more in control. John walked in and asked what my plans were for the afternoon.

"I might take Sydney into town."

"With your mom?"

"Probably not."

"I don't think that's a good idea," John whispered.

"Why are you whispering?"

"Shhh!"

The bathroom grew smaller, damp, claustrophobic. I heard footsteps outside, near the stairway. I wasn't sure whose they were, but I knew the most frightening sound in this house was a whisper.

"Why can't Sydney go into town with me?"

"That's not the part that's a bad idea," he said quietly.

"Send me a text," I said.

He reached into his pocket. I picked up my phone and watched as it came through.

I NEED TO WATCH UR DAD.
BUT YOU NEED TO WATCH UR MOM.

I texted back:

WHAT?

Then two photos came through.

A poster on the Brownsteins' property.
And scraps of newspaper on our kitchen table.

Tom

B y the time Dad woke up, John and I were both in fresh swim trunks and polo shirts, and he, even groggy, even befuddled by whatever Mom claimed was fucking with his brain, recognized that something fun was happening, and he agreed readily to take a walk.

We sat at the pier, and the earlier part of the day seemed very far away. Boats came and went along the harbor; parents wrestled squealing kids on the sand. Gaggles of bikers rang their bells in code, seagulls squawked, swings squeaked on the nearby playground, dogs barked for a Frisbee on the grass near the bandstand. If you listened carefully, you might even hear the lapping of ice cream cones, the slurping of iced coffees. Some afternoons, it seemed all of Nantucket passed by here on the way to town or the yacht club or the bike shop. Maybe the hubbub was a good thing. Maybe when you reached a certain age, a big swath of open beach sparked too much contemplation. It's possible stretches of sand made you worried that's what heaven was like, calm but empty. Who wants that?

Whatever the reasons, whatever the difference, the coconut aroma of sunscreen, the half-mossy, half-salty tang of the dock— it all seemed to soothe him. This was the thing we sometimes forgot—that most of the time, Dad was perfectly fine.

Then we walked home, and I saw it first, saw it as we approached our front lawn, the strange indentation, near the hedge, like crop circles. Dark and light. Light and dark.

I lifted my sunglasses onto my head, as if their tint was obscuring my vision. I stopped, and my dad ran into my shoulder blade, a pileup of sorts.

"Jesus Christ," I said. "Is that what I think it is?"

The Barrett's tour bus rumbled slowly down Hulbert Avenue, the guide talking loudly enough that we could hear her through the windows. "Hulbert Avenue is home to some of Nantucket's oldest summer homes. Designed with no winterized features, they—"

One by one, the cameras appeared, along with the gasps.

A swastika, mowed into our lawn.

"Move it!" I cried out. "Move the goddamn bus!"

I banged my fist above the taillight, over and over, till I thought I could dent it, punch through the metal.

I looked over my shoulder for John and my dad. They were together, thank God. John's arm on my father's. I saw them in a kind of slow motion, or maybe I just remembered it that way, had to slow it down to take it in. My brother-in-law reaching up to pull my father's right arm down, tucking Dad's limbs tight to his ribs to keep him safe, or maybe, just maybe, to keep him from saluting, from turning this horrible mistake into something awful and true.

Caroline

T he first thing I did was run down into the basement and look for the tarps.

The basement floor was dirt, soft and cold underfoot, comforting, somehow, even in my sweaty workout clothes—or when I was barefoot and in pajamas, hiding from my family, as I used to do as a child. I'd hear them running around upstairs, dropping things, clunking golf clubs. Nobody even looking for me. I went downstairs to stay cool, to stay away. And to listen. You could hear everything in that house. There was no insulation, no ductwork, no thick plaster keeping us away from one another. Just thin slices of wood. Windows open. Breezes blew through and brought all the noises of the harbor and the houses straight in, whether we wanted them or not. Foghorns, waves crashing on rocks. But also wailing babies, laughing houseguests, sizzling steaks. You heard everything, always, in that house, on that block, and that was the part that no one could understand. If I had been telling the truth about the night in the tent, wouldn't someone have heard it all?

Now, I heard a siren coming closer, my father's voice rising in the backyard.

Matt didn't have to tend to the basement, but he always did. Hauled anything rusty to the dump, put it all back as orderly as a hardware store, with bins and shelves, hanging on pegboards like with like. After he used the tarps and drop cloths, he folded them as carefully as my mother folded my father's T-shirts. Smoothing them, I imagined, with some memory lingering in his hand.

I grabbed two green ones and two brown ones and looked for some cord to lash them together. I opened a workbench drawer, and there it was. A bag of stakes and rings from the old tent. It was like looking at an evidence locker in a police station. There it is. Proof. As if the canvas and metal could give up the story.

When I pulled out the bag, the edge of something else caught my eye. I reached in, scrabbled around. Knew it the moment I felt it. A wooden keychain in the shape of a heart. Matt had made it for me, all those years ago, and I'd thrown it back in his face. I still remember the trajectory of it flying through the air and the clang when it hit the rim of his aviators. Here was his heart. Sanded and curved. Right next to the tent. I stood there a minute, considered what it meant, that he didn't want to throw it away but didn't want to keep it with him. Then I closed the drawer and ran up the wooden stairs, rattling them with each step.

Outside, I moved quickly. The indented pattern in the lawn already looked brown—raw and angry. It would darken for a few days, then start to grow again. But how long would it take?

Covering up was my instinct, not call the police (Tom's), not get a hotel room (Sydney's), not dig it up and lay down some sod (Mom's). Not screw 'em, who cares, it's our lawn (Dad's). No, first things first. We tarp it so we don't have to look at it, and the neighbors don't have to look at it, and then we figure out all the rest. We'd come home just minutes after the boys, from another direction, walking back from Cliff Road, to find the three of them arguing on the porch about what to do.

That left John to answer Sydney's questions, and Tom to deal with Dad, and no one to deal with Mom, but Mom had already done enough damage. It seemed like a simple equation: She'd called him a Jew. He'd called her a Nazi. She'd done it quietly; he'd done it showily. It hadn't yet occurred to me that anyone would know this but John. No detective had seen the newspaper and scissors on our kitchen table. No detective knew that Bear Brownstein wanted us to take down our widow's walk.

John came out and helped me string the tarps together, then pound them into the ground. We were almost finished when a police car pulled into our driveway. I didn't see who it was until he stepped out, the full height of him, unfolding out of the car like a knife. Billy Clayton.

He looked around in all directions as he walked toward us, even seemed to sniff the air like a dog, as if he could smell death, trouble, conspiracy.

He shaded his eyes with his hand. "Hello, Caroline."

"Hi, Billy."

"Billy Clayton," he said, extending his hand to John.

"Detective?" John asked.

"Lieutenant."

I raised my mallet to drive another stake into the soft grass, and Billy cleared his throat and told me I needed to stop.

"Stop?"

"Yes."

"I think someone else needs to stop."

He smiled. "You haven't changed a bit in all these years, you know that?"

"Oh, I think I have," I said, lifting my mallet. "I'm stronger."

"Caroline, I know you're angry, and this is terrible, but I need this all to come off so I can see it, take photos, gather evidence."

"There's no evidence needed. Bear Brownstein did it."

"Well, down at the police station, we enjoy having proof of these things."

"Fine," I said. "Then you can tear it apart, put it together again, and drive all the stakes back in."

"All right," he said calmly.

"Help yourself," I said. I threw the tools down and walked away.

I watched from inside as he unfurled the tarp, rolling it carefully along one edge, like he was the caretaker of a stadium field. He stood on the hood of his car and angled his camera to get the best view. *The tour bus view,* I thought. And I wondered, suddenly, heartbreakingly, if you could see this from the top deck of the ferry. Steaming in toward a day or weekend of fun, was this what you saw first in the harbor?

John followed me inside.

"What did you tell Sydney?"

"Oh," he said. "She already knew."

"Knew what?"

"Knew what a swastika was, what it signified. She gets A's in history, remember."

"No, John," I said, irritation rising in my throat. "What do you tell her about our family? About why it's on our lawn?"

"I told her it was illegal, and it was based on a mistake."

"A mistake?"

"Yes, that they mistook a German heritage for a Nazi heritage."

"Did she ask any questions?"

"Yes, she said, 'If Mom is half German and you are zero parts German, what does that make me?'"

Now it was my turn to smile. "I guess we'll be getting her a math tutor."

"Where's your mom?" he asked suddenly.

"She's with Tom and Dad."

He paused. "I emptied it, by the way."

"Emptied what?"

"The recycling. I took the newspaper scraps to the Dumpster at Children's Beach this morning."

"That was prescient. I suppose if Duffy the Crime Dog finds that out, he'll think you did it."

John shrugged. "Will you visit me in prison?"

I smiled despite myself. "It's not funny, you know."

"I know. But it's interesting how we keep saying that, because we just keep finding the humor in it. But the police are involved now. Brownstein took it too far, and he'll be the one blamed, not your mother for starting it, but him for escalating."

"How do you know?"

"What she did was nothing compared to this."

"Do you think so?"

"I do," he said, and I looked into his eyes, solemn and dark, as brown as they were green, like a glistening pond you discover in the woods. And I believed him.

Maggie Sue

I t was just luck that I was there again. He'd sent me home
when I'd found the flyer, then called later and asked me to
come back the next day. He knew better than this, really. It was
July, and I was booked solid, even working Saturdays. I drew the
line at Sundays, fearing God would strike me dead if I dared show
my head in St. Mary's smelling of Scrubbing Bubbles instead of
bubble bath. You can complain about Catholic doctrine all you
want, but resting on Sunday, well, there's something to that. A
walk on the beach, a long bath. Sometimes I cook something
that takes forever, like baked beans or a short rib. But you won't
catch me cleaning. Oh no. Not even dishes. Sunday evenings, I
lay in the hammock in the shade of my little porch, a thick layer
of Eucerin soaking into my hands, trying to take away the damage
of the week.

So no, I'd told him I couldn't, that I had two other houses
that day, and he'd asked me if I could rearrange something, come
early. He said please. He didn't mention money, but I sensed there
would be money involved if I changed things, and I was right.
Sixty extra dollars in the envelope on the counter. Part of me was
hoping for a hundred, I'll admit, but another part was just glad it
wasn't twenty. Twenty and I would have lost respect for the man.
I'd hurried on my other two jobs so I could get here before sunset,

add his in, so that was worth more than twenty, that hustling. I was hot and sticky, and I'd skipped lunch.

I worked from the top down, as always. Upstairs, nothing looked out of place. His bathroom rarely had anything but a few drops of water in the sink. No mess in the toilet, ever, no towels on the floor. Someone else did his laundry, I knew, at Holdgate's. I'd seen the bags delivered in the laundry room. And he always said to leave the sheets in there, not the towels. I did what I was told, because that was the most important part of the job—following instructions. Just like they tell you in third grade. Before you take the test, read the instructions.

I had finished Windexing the mirrors and was working on the chrome fixtures in the first-floor powder room. That was my favorite part of my job, although it's funny to say that. I like the way silver bits can go so quick from dull to shiny—how you can take off the layer of toothpaste and hairspray and liquid soap, and part of the bathroom shines like jewelry again. Before I leave a room, I always do the same to the doorknob too. Just as I finished doing that, I saw Billy Clayton through the window of the front door, before he knocked. He looked me square in the eyes and raised his, instead of knocking. I let him in.

"Wiping off fingerprints?" he said.

"It's called cleaning."

"Not in my line of work," he said, flicking his badge with his fingers. It looked dull in the light, like he'd dripped toothpaste or soda on it. If I liked Billy better, I might've offered to shine that too.

"Well, that's what normal people call it. You should try it sometime."

"How you been, Maggie?"

"Oh, dandy. How 'bout yourself?"

"Fine, thanks. Didn't know you worked for Mr. Brownstein every day."

"Didn't know you cared what I did."

"Well, do you?"

"Do I what?"

"Work for him every day?"

"No."

"And yet here you are, again. He told me you were the one who found the poster. Spelled your name for me correctly and everything."

"Billy, what the hell you want this time? You have some news about what I found, or—"

"Do you have any news for *me* about what you found?"

I put down my rag and sighed. Billy was nice enough looking, if you squinted. If you could get past the hard facade of all the angles of his chin, the ledge of his eyebrows, the comb marks in his hair. All lines and corners, that one, his whole face a geometry lesson.

"No, but if I did, I'd call you."

"Would you?"

"Billy, I got a house to clean! Get to the fucking point!"

"Was Mr. Brownstein home at all since you've been here today?"

"No."

"You sure?"

"Pretty sure."

"What do you mean?"

"I mean, I've been upstairs using water, flushing toilets, and squeaking a rag around, but I didn't hear him come home."

"But he could have."

"Christ on a cracker. If you wanna give me the runaround, you can start running the vacuum around and be helpful."

I tossed the microfiber cloth in the laundry room, got another clean one from the drawer in the kitchen, and when I came back to the living room, he was still exactly where he'd been. His eyes followed me as if there was some knowledge hidden in my limbs. Was I dusting guiltily? Spraying furniture oil in a pattern that suggested I was hiding something?

"Did you drive by the Warners' on your way here today?"

"I don't remember."

"Well, if you came from home—"

"I didn't come from home. I came from another job. No."

"No what?"

"No, I didn't go by."

"You just remembered that?"

"Yeah, because I came down the Cliff, came from the other direction."

"You mind telling me which house you were at on the Cliff?"

"What, you going to arrest me now? Is that it? You following my whereabouts?"

"Just doing my job."

"Reilly."

"What?"

"Reilly. That's where I came from. The Reillys', out near Madaket Marine."

"I don't know them."

"What a shame. They have a pool, and a hot college-age daughter."

If he was getting impatient with me, it was impossible to tell. That was his superpower, his poker face.

He continued to watch me dust the table, the wooden edges of the chairs, the picture frames. It had to be boring, but he was just biding his time. We were at a kind of stalemate now, two quiet people waiting to hear what they needed to hear.

"If you think you're just gonna wait here till he comes home," I said finally, "you're gonna hafta wait in your squad car."

"Why's that?"

"Because you don't have a warrant to be here."

"Don't need to have a warrant for a friendly chat."

"I'm not authorized to let people in."

"He doesn't let you offer a friend a glass of water when you're working?"

"We're not friends, Billy."

"Was there a gardening crew here or anywhere on the street when you arrived?"

"Nope."

"Are there gardening tools in the shed? Mowers, weed whackers?"

"No idea."

"Was it possible Mr. Brownstein was in the backyard, perhaps, when you arrived?"

"I told you—"

"You hear any rustling perhaps? Trees moving, equipment being dragged, anything going through the bushes, maybe cutting through to the Warners'?"

"Why do you come to the Brownsteins' but keep asking me about the Warners? I can barely see them from here!"

"Their property was defaced."

"Defaced? Like with paint?"

"No, like with a mower."

"A lawn mower?"

"Looks like it, from the size of it."

The smile on my lips just kept getting bigger until I started laughing. I imagine I looked demonic, cleaning and laughing. Laughing and cleaning. But it felt good. It's therapeutic, it really is, doing both at the same time. Like singing and cleaning, same thing.

"It's not funny, Maggie. Someone mowed a swastika on their lawn. It's a hate crime."

"Well, I'm sorry, but—"

"But what?"

"You don't really think Bear Brownstein has ever mowed a lawn in his life, do you?"

"It's not that hard to mow a—"

"The man cannot hang a picture, okay? There is no hammer or screwdriver in this house."

"What?"

"You heard me. No tools. He's a geek. Totally, utterly inept. Hires Marine Home Center to come and hang pictures."

"Anyone can hang a picture."

"The man cannot hang a picture. I'm telling ya. I'm giving you useful information now, and you wanna argue with me. Classic."

"Well, then, fine, all right. The man can't mow a lawn. Maybe he used a weed whacker."

"Billy, you're killing me. This is a man who probably can't turn on an electric knife, let alone a weed whacker."

"Well, maybe he hired someone to do it."

"What, you think he found and hired an angry Jewish grounds-keeper to do his dirty work? You think that's possible?"

"I think anything's possible."

"You'd have to, to follow your theory. You'd have to believe there are dinosaurs roamin' the old golf course."

"You know what I think?"

"I think you're going to tell me what I think," I said and sighed.

"I think you like this guy."

"It's time for you to go," I said, feeling my cheeks flush. I walked to the front door, opened it, gestured.

"I think you'd lie for him if he asked you to. I know you were prone to that in your youth."

Now my face was on fire. My Irish coming up, my dad used to say, but it had nothing to do with where I was born or how much I had to drink. It was anger, fury, pure and simple. How dare he? I hadn't lied, those years ago. *I'd been mistaken.* There was a difference, and he knew it.

"Is it a hate crime to tell a cop to go fuck himself? Just wondering."

"Well," he said as he went outside, "it's a crime to conceal evidence for someone. You can get away with it when you're a juvenile. But you're an adult now, aren't you, Maggie?"

"Go fuck yourself, Billy," I said. I closed the door and snapped the deadbolt shut. His face through the glass of the window was just as calm, just as unwrinkled as the sea at low tide. Giving nothing up, ever. Just waiting.

Well, he could wait forever, because I knew nothing. I knew worthless things, like what kind of toothpaste Bear used, and what kind of mug he liked. I knew what was in his house, but not what was in his heart. The man lived as if he were in a model home, not a real home. Like he was just passing through, cutting through the lawns like he did, on the way to someplace else.

Alice

I should have left him the moment I found out his father was a Nazi.

Wouldn't that have been dramatic? That's how it would have happened in a film or a book. Not in real life. No, in real life, there's lack of movement, misplaced loyalty. Hope. Optimism. And regret.

People who claim regrets, late in life, usually talk about small things, about going outside more often on sunny days, about pushing their children on the swings, about indulging their "one more times!" instead of saying enough. Why? Because those regrets seem fixable when they see them in others. Say yes instead of no. Eat the dessert. Give the hug. Wear the purple hat with feathers. Don't bitterly turn away from miniature possibilities.

But what of the big regrets? Of knowing, suddenly, that Tripp wasn't who I thought he was. I could have overlooked the sins of his father, his grandfather. But that he would lie, would gloss over it all, would try to pass himself off as something else. I never trusted him after that, and that was the truth.

Well, it's never too late. It's never too late to cut them loose. Especially when they are about to become a drain on resources. But speaking of regrets, when you are a septuagenarian on vacation and call your lawyer to discuss initiating divorce proceedings, don't do it in a house with thin walls. Or you will surely regret hanging up the phone and finding your daughter in the corridor, her face a mask of red fury.

Caroline grabbed my arm with a ferocity I always knew she had—squeezed my delicate wrist with such force, I thought she'd snap it. Wasn't that what I'd told the officers all those years ago? That she could murder any one of those boys with one hand tied behind her back? That if everything she claimed was true, they'd be scratched and bruised far more than she was?

"You called a divorce lawyer?"

My other arm scrabbled behind me for the wall. My nails dug into the old wallpaper and the thin plaster underneath. All of it insubstantial, every layer.

"Let go of me," I said evenly.

"What do you think you're doing, Mom?"

"What I probably should have done years before. Figuring out my options."

"Are you kidding me?"

"I should think about protecting you."

"Me?"

"Well, and Sydney, of course. And Tom."

"From what?"

The star-shaped, silver light fixture swung above my head. Dust motes swirled in front of my eyes, tiny and beautiful, like something they were not.

Our tussle had jostled and weakened the whole house.

She let go of my arm, and I rubbed it gratefully.

"From the asset-drain of his long-term, twenty-four-hour care. Don't you want to inherit some money?"

"Mother, Dad needs you now. Don't you—"

"I have at least ten good years left. Ten, Caroline. Or who knows, possibly more. My family has huge amounts of longevity in their DNA. And ten years is an eternity. I'm not going to waste them being married to an imbecile who no longer understands which way is up. Or to someone everyone now knows has Nazi lineage. I can pretend I just found out, that he confessed, that I haven't known all along and hid it for him."

"Mom, what are you say—"

"I found out a week before our wedding, and I should have called it off right then and there. It was an omen. Do you have any idea how exhausting it all was? Being married, having children with—"

"Of course I do. I have a chil—"

"But you have John! I had no John. I had your father, who did nothing, in case you didn't notice. Oh, good time Charlie he was. All about playing catch and having treats. But he did nothing! You of all people should know he did nothing, even when it mattered most."

Did her lower lip quiver then? Or did I just imagine it? I'd heard her little friend that summer, in those in-between weeks when a few girls were still on her side, saying that *her father would have killed those boys.* Would have *murdered them with his bare hands.* How must that have felt, that inaction? Her ally, unallied. Oh well, she had John now. She had her own little family to hang on her every word, believe in whatever she told them. She could twist it all to her advantage now; she didn't need anyone else. And that's what memory does, does it not? Preserves it all like a bug trapped in your own resin, making it whatever you wish.

"Dad is German, but lots of people are German. They—"

"His father was SS!"

"Grandpa?"

"Changed his name from Werner to Warner."

Footsteps on the stairs, half running, and then, hesitation. We both stopped talking, waiting. What were they doing halfway up, where we couldn't see them? Who was it? I heard them turn, go down again. Only John would have the sense to do that. It must have been John.

"That's impossible. They track those people down. They could never—"

"Suit yourself, Caroline. Believe whatever you wish."

"Did Grandma know?"

"Of course she knew. But she was a different generation. They were more understanding. They knew how easy it was to get caught up."

"Caught up?"

"Caroline, just imagine for a second what it was like to live in Germany back then! They had no options. It was get with the program or get out!"

"But Grandpa's money—"

"He made that here."

"With what? How do you buy real estate unless you have funds?"

"Do I really have to spell it out for you? He stole! He took artwork, silver, who knows what all. Oh, don't look so shocked. Naïveté does not become you."

"It's just, I'm stunned. I feel as if—"

I held up a hand. "If you say your entire life has been a lie, I swear, Caroline, I will vomit right on your shoes."

"Mother, you have to admit it's disconcerting. It's like finding out you were adopted! Your family is not who they say they are."

"Well, now you have another reason to hate your family. Are you happy?"

"I don't hate anyone."

Oh, the look on her face as she said that! Vitriol filling her from within! Her anger was the only thing that kept her going, and she didn't have any idea.

Own it, Caroline, I wanted to say. *Just admit that nothing has turned out as you expected it to, that everyone you love has disappointed you. Own it, as I have.*

"Well, now that Bear Brownstein has told the world, what do you suppose he'll do next?"

"Mom, you need to end this."

"End it? So that…that…*kike* can have the upper hand and go do something else? Maybe carve the word 'rape' into the back lawn. How would you like that?"

"Jesus, Mom," Caroline said. "Are you sure you're not the fucking Nazi?"

She turned and walked away.

I think Tripp, an only child of only children, his parents both gone, was searching for connection when he first starting digging around. He found a scattering of his mother's relatives, who were English and Irish and lived in Boston. But there was nothing he could find about his father. A librarian suggested perhaps there'd been a name change, and he'd gone to Ellis Island, perhaps knowing in his heart what was about to happen, remembering his father cooking him spaetzle whenever he was ill and bringing home stollen at Christmas. His friends never ate such things. One letter. One quick change, and there it was. *Werner to Warner.*

Caroline had never expressed much interest in her heritage; she was so sullen as a teenager, always bickering with her brother. She wanted her own family, not ours. She wanted to create a future and leave us all in the dust. And I wonder what she would think if she knew what I knew about my own cousins in France, who they harbored, what they risked.

Does that make up for it? And why can't I be more like them, harboring the stranger, the fugitive who is now my husband?

Tom

I was jolted awake by my sister, and it felt as annoying as it was familiar. All those Christmas mornings when she was up first. The family road trips, when everyone else was waiting in the car, and she was sent back in to wake me up. When I was younger, I wondered if Caroline ever slept at all.

"What?" I asked when she barged into my room. The way she walked, the smell of her hair. I knew it wasn't my father standing in the threshold, that's for sure.

"Oh, you're awake?"

"I am now."

"Get up. There's a fire."

"In the house?" I sat up quickly, grabbed my shirt and khakis, crumpled from the night before. She turned her back at the sight of my blue boxers.

"No, outside," she said and left.

I got dressed, ran downstairs. Outside could mean anywhere, and from our porch, we could almost certainly see it. A boat explosion in the harbor, kitchen fire at the White Elephant, arson at the lighthouse, terrorism at Brant Point Naval Station. But I knew, instinctively, exactly where it was.

In the kitchen, in the living room, all the doors, usually wide open, were closed against the smoke and ash. John and Caroline argued in the kitchen, struggling to keep their voices down.

"Where's everyone else?"

"Asleep," Caroline said.

"Alice isn't asleep," John said.

I went to the back kitchen door and looked out. Flames in the outline of a house, like some kind of symbol or magic trick, a hoop you could jump through. It appeared as if it would burn itself out quickly; there was nothing else on that side of the lot to burn—no trees or grass. Just the framing set in concrete.

The fire truck sirens blasted around the corner; flashing lights lit up the block. We all heard their shouted instructions, the step of their heavy boots, the dragging of their hoses.

"Work men with cigarettes?" I said to no one in particular. "Kids smoking pot? Fireworks?" My voice was hopeful.

"Mom said he probably did it himself, for the insurance money," Caroline said.

"When did she say that?"

"When I went in to wake her."

"She was already awake, though, wasn't she?" John asked.

"What?"

"Did she smell like smoke? Like kerosene?"

"John!"

"Well, everything smells here now," I said, sniffing.

"She was down here, late last night. I left her right here, with a full pot of tea, staring out at his house."

"Oh, for God's sake, John. That doesn't mean anything."

"This cat-and-mouse game the two of them are playing—"

"He's playing, but we don't really know what she's done."

"I told you, I saw the newspaper scraps. And if the detective did any investigating at all, he probably saw me ferrying them away too."

"What paper?" I said.

"The cut-up newspaper," John said. "From the poster."

"So you made it? John, you surprise me."

"Very funny."

It wasn't funny, but I didn't want to think my mother was that childish and that petty. However, there was one thing I was sure of: John was not a liar.

"Well, a note of warning is not the same as arson," Caroline said. "Everything on this island is made of wood. How many times did Mom tell us that, did she yell at Tom and Dad to put out their cigars? I just...I just can't see it. I can't."

"Caroline, that man is either over there right now telling the firefighters that your mother burned down his pool house, or he's planning his retaliation, or both."

"Well, what do you want me to do about it, John?"

"I think we should send Matt over there to negotiate," I said.

"Matt's not family," she spat out.

"Precisely."

"Speaking of the newspaper," I said, picking up the one on a kitchen chair. We stared at the front page together.

Hate crimes rock Hulbert Avenue residents

Two properties along Brant Point have been vandalized in what police are investigating as potential hate crimes this week. An anti-Semitic poster was found on Robert Brownstein's Henry Street property while under renovation, and a Nazi symbol was found on Thomas Warner III's lawn when his family returned after an outing.

The investigation is ongoing, and police are unwilling to say whether the events are linked. But both beachgoers and homeowners have expressed shock and fear.

"I've never locked my doors before," one resident, who wished to remain anonymous, said. "But I'm locking them now."

Matt

I didn't tell my wife I was going back to the Warners'.

It was almost dawn, early even for me, and before I got Tom's text, I heard the sirens and knew, instinctively, that the trouble came from their house. My wife didn't say anything when I told her I had to go; she just sighed. As if she knew and just didn't want to deal with it anymore. If she thought about it for even a half a second, she'd realize that family needed me, needed me always, and not be upset. Or jealous. Or whatever irrational feeling might storm through her now and then where they were concerned. Never said anything, but we both felt it.

It's hard for her. Me being a native, knowing everyone through all these summers. She's just as pretty as Caroline, but I don't know if she knows that. I saw her once, checking out Caroline's Facebook page, scrolling through the few photos that were there. Looking for something she probably couldn't find. She's from Florida, came here one summer to waitress, escaping the heat, following the lead of scores of workers who split time between two glorious locations. She met me a month before she was due to leave, and then she stayed. Said she preferred the cooler temperatures, but we both knew what was going on. It hadn't been a long time for me between dates, but it had been a long time between girlfriends. She had a quiet strength about her that was familiar, but a warmth to her smile that was new. She was a contradiction. And we'd never talked much about Caroline, but it's hard to keep secrets on this island. I wondered, always, if she knew the full truth.

When I met her, I sat at the bar of the Galley, drinking an eighteen-dollar cocktail just so I could watch her carry three plates down an arm or hoist two pitchers of water like it was nothing. Or maybe I just wanted to watch her shimmy past the tables in the tight skirt and striped T-shirt they all wore. She and I still go there sometimes for old time's sake—usually in September, on a Thursday when it's not too busy, just to toast our old haunt and say hello to the busboys or anyone who's around. I don't pay for my drinks when she's with me. The manager still remembers her and knows we recommend the restaurant to all my clients. *Expensive but worth every penny*, I say. *The only place with tables on the beach. Like South Beach without all the people.*

I'm careful with my words. I think about what I say now, with clients, with my wife, with the Warners. Especially with Caroline. I learned my lesson. Measure twice, because it cuts once.

Two fire trucks when I arrived, plus a police car. Their candy lights pulsed out of time with each other, almost festive, like a honky-tonk, a kind of neon light you don't see often on our subtle island, where store signs are made of wood and lighting falls under zoning laws. A few people lined the streets in pajamas and thrown-on workout gear, watching a whole lot of nothing. It was clear the moment I got out of my truck that this was a fire that would burn itself out and not risk a single tree or home, but they pulled out a hose anyway and wet it down completely, not taking a chance with an errant spark. Not in a town made of wood, bark, and petal.

Tom Warner stood at the edge of the property, facing the street, not the fire, eyes cast down. He scraped his toe where the grass trailed off into sandy dirt, like he was writing his name in it.

Up on the porch, Caroline and her husband sat beneath the

porch light, as if they wanted to be seen. She gestured to him with her hands, and he nodded. *Good*, I wanted to say; agreeing with her is always the right stance to take.

"Not a great week for Hulbert Avenue," I said to Tom as I walked up.

"You can say that again."

"I tried to go over, Tom, but Billy Clayton told me to leave, that it was a crime scene. Couldn't even see Brownstein through the window. I don't know if he's hiding or what."

"Maybe I should go over," Tom said and sighed. "Do you think he'd punch me? Or would I punch him first?"

"I'm not sure I'd be that gracious, Tom, to try and talk."

"I don't know that anyone has ever called me gracious."

"I was talking about him. Fire could have been anything, though. Job site like that. He should know that."

He looked at me with a half smile on his face. I was familiar with that look; it reminded me of his sister. As if a whole smile was too much to give just anyone. You had to earn the rest of it.

"You don't really believe that," Tom said.

"I do."

"Well, if you talk to John, you won't."

"He thinks Tripp escaped with a box of matches, huh?"

"No. Mom."

"Alice?"

To say I was incredulous was an understatement. She was a strong-willed woman, for sure, but setting a fire? Regardless of how she felt about Brownstein, that was like risking her own property, others, her neighborhood. I couldn't see it. Not a dyed-in-the-wool Nantucketer. No.

"She's guilty of some stuff, that's for sure, but I don't know," Tom said and sighed. "I don't know anymore."

"What are you going to do?"

"I guess leave. But the hotels are all probably booked this weekend. Maybe we could find something on Airbnb."

"Let me check around. One of my clients might have an unrented cottage. Might be small, but something."

"Thanks, Matt."

"How's Caroline holding up?"

Tom looked back at the porch. We stood there together, watching her talk to her husband, as if it was somehow interesting to watch two people doing nothing.

"Oh, you know Caroline. She's always fine, and yet never fine, you know. But John makes things better."

"Does he?"

"Don't mistake her coldness for sadness, man."

"I didn't th—"

"She's happy with him."

"Again, I wasn't suggest—"

"Yes, you were," he said and laughed. "Looking for an opening, right? A crack in the foundation."

"No."

He clasped my shoulder and told me it was okay, we all had our obsessions. I'd never thought of Caroline as an obsession. She was more like a path through the woods that you remember from your childhood, exactly as it was. Dappled and cool, moss underfoot, restful and familiar. You don't want to see something you've loved with such tenderness be overgrown, gone forever.

"Tom, did you ever ask your neighbors about those video cameras across the street?"

"No."

"I wonder if Billy has now, to see who carved up your lawn."

"I fucking hope he didn't," he said. "Or maybe they taped over already. Let's hope they did."

"Why?"

"Because God only knows what they'd show Alice doing."

I allowed myself to think of it then, just for a minute. To imagine Alice Warner arrested, handcuffed, in a jail cell. What she would say. The demands she would make. And how that tough old bird wouldn't tell anyone anything useful, even if she were waterboarded.

Caroline

I know Matt's just trying to be helpful. That's what John said when he saw my body tense, and of course he's right. Just because I don't want his help anymore, that doesn't mean that Matt wasn't born to be helpful, to be useful, and that he always tried to do the right thing even when he did the wrong thing. If Matt ever broke the law, ever lied, ever hurt someone, it was for good reason. Everyone knew this about him; it was why he was the most popular caretaker on the island. A job he was born to. A job he could have performed magnificently, even when he was young. When he tried to fix me.

When he looks at me now, though, I can't meet his gaze. There is a searching in it, as if he's surveying me, trying to find the loose floorboard, the hanging hinge. I want to tell him that I'm fine, that he can leave it. I guess his wife is too healthy, too whole; Matt always needs a project, a wounded bird. That, or maybe he is unhappy. How am I to know? I don't want to get too close to him to find out. When he walks in, I can still smell the tang of his lime deodorant, the familiar scent of his neck. You can love another man and be perfectly happy, and still be lured by another scent. You can. I know it. But the scent can be false. The scent can be empty as salt and sugar once they leave your tongue. In Matt's case, it was like opening a drawer and smelling the dark and earthy aroma of my youth.

But this time, he really was helpful. The gratitude in my mother's eyes is the rarest sight in the world, and he sparked it. Found a client whose rental had canceled in a house on Dix Street, one of the short lanes tucked around the corner from our house.

John helped my mother pack up my father's things. I left him in the master bedroom while I packed ours and Sydney's. Tom threw all our bags into the trunk of his car and drove the three blocks while the rest of us walked. The cottage was in an ideal location, considering. My father could walk to the same beach in front of our house and to Jetties for lunch and almost feel as though he was at the same place. But we wouldn't have to see our own house or walk by the Brownsteins'.

Dad had been confused by the hubbub, couldn't seem to remember what a swastika was or the name of the man who lived behind us. When Tom had said, "He's upset because he's Jewish," Dad had thought he'd said "fluish."

The cottage had three bedrooms plus a sleeping porch with a daybed that sagged a bit in the middle. Tom bounced on it, testing its springs, then offered to take it, since he stayed up the latest, drinking bourbon and smoking cigars in any outdoor location available. I told him fine, but he had to wake up earlier now, because the family needed somewhere to gather for coffee and the paper.

"You can't *gather* in the kitchen?" He mocked me on the word *gather* as if it was foreign, snobby, accented.

"Dad likes being outside."

We stood together, surveying the small backyard through the screen. Ours was the middle cottage in a trio, each small, old but well maintained. On the left, the yard held traces of construction—a sawhorse, a Dumpster. On the right, a brick patio with two Adirondack chairs. A tall hedge shielded all three from the neighboring property, which spanned all of the backyards. Three lots. The neighbor had three lots.

"Oh, come on," he said. "You're using Dad as an excuse for everything now."

"It's only a few days."

"It's five days, actually. If I make it that long."

"If *you* make it that long? Is that what you said?"

"Well, you've appointed me Dad's jailer, and now you and John have decided Mom needs a bodyguard too. I've got two hands and two eyes and one week of vacation, and I think everybody's overreacting just a smidge."

"You sound just like Mom."

"What the hell is that supposed to fucking mean?"

I don't think I'd ever seen him get that angry that quickly. Tom was usually more a low-level kind of permanently pissed-off type, defaulting to grumpy, ignoring what he wanted to in order to preserve his precious status quo. It's like he was both above and beneath anger.

"Oh, I'm sorry. Does that threaten your precious masculinity? Are you afraid I'm suggesting you've gone soft like an old woman?"

"You don't get it," he said.

"Oh really? What don't I get, Tom?"

"You're not the only one who's been hurt by her."

My mouth hung open. I felt like I was in some kind of alternate universe.

"Oh, it must have been awful all these years, being her favorite, being her precious firstborn prince! You poor thing!"

"You don't know anything, Caroline."

He walked away from me like he always does, to all of us. I'd been staring at the back of his blond head, the slight curve in his shoulders, my whole life.

"I know this much," I yelled after him. "I've had it, okay? There's a fucking rapist loose on the island, and from now on, the only person I'm watching is my daughter. You got that?"

"Fine," he shouted over his shoulder.

The most commonly spoken word between us, always.

Tom

Something to think about when you're planning your family: the worst combination is one boy and one girl. Why don't people see that? Everyone wants two, one of each, so they can experience the full spectrum. But that's the loneliest way to go. That's the most dangerous way to go.

My mother pitted us against each other like dogs; I see that now. The competition was meant to ramp up our affection for her, and for a while, it worked on my end. Never on Caroline's, though. She took it all personally, always. Only saw things from her own point of view. So poor Alice's strategy backfired, and she amped up the pressure on me. Bad move. I don't like pressure. I don't like being blamed for things I didn't do.

But still she hammers. When she called and asked me to come to Nantucket, when she said she needed our help and I told her I was too busy at work and to hire a local caregiver, she said, "You have to come. You can't do that to Caroline."

"I'm not doing it to Caroline."

"Indeed you are. Leaving her alone, just like you did in the tent."

"For God's sake, Mother. I didn't leave her alone in the goddamn tent!"

"If you hadn't flirted with those silly friends of hers, would they have been so eager to come inside?"

"That's not what happened! They were cold!"

"So they said."

"Jesus, Mom, this has nothing to do with that."

She quieted then, but her silence was only to let it all soak in. With my family, no matter what I do, no matter what I say, it's wrong. I try my best, and my best is just a little shittier than everyone else's, so there you have it. Sometimes I wonder if my dad was the same way. If he just resigned himself to always being wrong and always being less and just gave in to her, so he could have some peace. And she did grant him freedom, much of the time. My entire life, I can barely remember the two of them together except for at a meal. Different hobbies, different interests, even different friends. The way he said "the bridge gang" and she said "your golf buddies"—both of them with a whiff of derision, as if they were saying "Hells Angels" or something. And why not stay separate, if this is where life takes you anyway—one in a nursing home facility and the other tucked away at home. Why wouldn't my parents end up apart when they had always been that way?

I walk toward the beach, alone for the first time since I arrived on the island. Not with my dad, not with John, and not with my sister and her kid. Just me, just like it used to be. I walked down the public access path and then picked my way toward Brant Point along the shoreline, stepping over the pilings and dinghies and kayaks. I liked watching the ferries come and go and seeing the different boats and equipment. People don't realize the entire beach is public in Nantucket. The folks with homes on the shore don't own the sand or the water. Locals come down here all the time, during the day, during the night. Many, many parties and memories here.

The wind had picked up, and a couple of people were kiteboarding. The only folks on the beach were watching them, as I was. As they swooped and dipped over the waves, their bright equipment dancing, I sat down and thought, once again, about taking a few lessons. I loved the idea of being outside when it was rough and enjoying the beach when everybody else had abandoned it. The sky darkened a little. Rain was forecast for late in the day, but I never put too much stock in the weather report. On an island, things were always changing. When I felt a few fat drops on my hand and shoulder, I stood up and started walking back before the rain truly began.

I walked by the old Grinstaff house. I couldn't help wondering if they had a wine cellar and how obvious their choices probably were. I'd heard Connor was divorced, and I hadn't known his wife, but I did know he'd always been a douche bag, no matter what anyone said or didn't say. But being a douche bag is not against the law. However, having money and a shitty wine cellar ought to be a punishable crime.

The path to Hulbert Avenue was overgrown, so I didn't see the cab pulling up to our old house, or I might have stopped it. Might have nipped the whole situation in the bud. Instead, I stepped outside through the bushes and heard knocking and a voice calling, "Hello? Is anybody home?"

I walked past the tarps, up to our porch.

"Can I help you?"

"Are you Mr. Warner?" the girl asked. She had that weird combination you see in wealthy kids—young face but a worldly voice. Like a baby hooker who summered in France and wintered in Gstaad.

"Yes," I replied. "One of them."

She looked vulnerable and small, standing there on the enormous empty porch. I thought of the rapist, roaming the beaches, and suddenly Caroline being overprotective of her daughter made more sense. This is how they look when they're alone. Delicate. Breakable as glass.

"Who are you?"

"I'm Courtney."

"Courtney?"

"Sydney's friend."

I resisted the urge to say *Oh fuck*, but I'm sure my face registered a mix of shock and horror. The name was familiar now. I could hear it in the air, the two syllables cut in half, the pronunciation crisp. I'd heard it not from my niece, and not from my sister, but most unfortunately, from my father.

"It's a surprise," she whispered.

Yes, I agreed. It certainly is.

Caroline

The way things were going for my family, it's a wonder Tom wasn't arrested for human trafficking as he walked through town with a romper-clad teen, her pale-blue Longchamp bag slung over his shoulder.

I was in the kitchen and heard them coming before I saw them, the flip-flop of her Tori Burch sandals, the familiar clearing of his throat, from drinking too much wine and smoking too many cigars. I stared at them walking down the street for a second before realizing who Tom was with.

"Sydney!" I called out in a low growl. "Does Courtney's family vacation in Nantucket too?"

"No?"

"You didn't…invite her, did you? When Pop suggested it, and I said no?"

"No, Mom, why—"

She followed my gaze and looked back at me solemnly. "I swear I didn't, Mom."

"Dad!" I bellowed. "Mom!"

"What?" my mother asked, hurrying down the stairs with my father in tow.

"Maybe Dad can explain to us how Sydney's friend Courtney managed to get herself invited here to Nantucket?"

"Dang it!" my dad said. "It was supposed to be a surprise!"

He and Sydney walked outside and hugged the girl, my father talking loudly, volubly.

My brother came into the kitchen.

"Sorry to be the bearer of bad teenage tidings."

"Well, she'll have a playmate. That will make everything simpler," my mother said.

"Mom, it makes nothing simpler!"

"Why on earth not?"

"Because Dad is ill! Because we're not in our house. Because we have no room!"

"Oh, we can always go back to the house."

"Mother, we are not going back to the house! No one is setting foot over there until the yard is dug up and the sod is delivered!"

"Well, there's plenty of room here," she said with a wave of her hand. "They're children! They can sleep in a tent on the lawn!"

I felt my brother's eyes move from my mother to me. I locked gazes with him and felt something I haven't felt in decades: complicity.

"The girls can have the porch if you like," Tom said. "I'll bunk on the couch."

"Thank you," I say quietly.

"You're welcome."

Tom

The evening passed without incident. John and I occupied
Dad with card games and Frisbee on the lawn while my sister
and mother cooked and did the dishes.

After everyone went to bed, I opened up a book and lay on
the couch with a pillow and an extra blanket. The girls were still
whispering on the porch with a flashlight. I heard Caroline and
John brushing their teeth, taking turns spitting, sharing the sink.

She came down in her pajamas, the same kind she's always
had, pastel prints, always too big for her. She doesn't like change.
Neither of us do, like our parents.

She pulled two chairs from the living room over to the screen
door that leads to the porch. Put her feet on one and sat on the
other. She leaned back and closed her eyes.

"What are you doing?" I said.

"Parenting."

"They're fine," I say.

"Oh, you're a parent now? You're an expert?"

I sighed. That's all, one exhalation.

"I'm sorry, am I interrupting your reading by being nearby? Does
my very existence keep you from your deep presleep thoughts?"

"This is ridiculous. The girls are home, not out on the beach
running wild. They're fine. I'm right here."

She laughs, a small quiet ripple that grows in intensity, until it's almost infectious. I smile.

It's been years, it seems, since I've heard my sister genuinely laugh.

Alice

Not everyone loves July 4 on Main Street. God knows some of our friends avoid it as if it were the plague. Staying inside, shades pulled low, flicking the pages of the *Inquirer Mirror* with distaste at every hoot or holler. But if this isn't the real America, children and dogs and musicians and shopkeepers all mixing on a cobblestone street, what is? The hordes of tiny flag-painted faces. The blueberry ice cream running down wrists. The star-spangled water guns, the street music, the fire truck standing by to douse the crowd at noon. And the crush, the sheer volume of people inching along is just the small price we pay.

Tripp and I had always appreciated the hubbub. Some traditions aren't easy; that doesn't make them any less worth doing. You want a clam, you have to dig it. To enjoy a bonfire, you have to gather the wood.

We'd taken Sydney every year since she was a baby, even in a stroller. And of course she wanted to go! We all did, even Tom.

The stores had been preparing for weeks, of course, setting up window and sidewalk displays. Most of the day-trippers would come later, streaming off the boats and walking straight up Main Street, here for afternoon shopping, dinner, and the fireworks, not the daytime festivities. No. Complain about it all you like, but this morning at least, downtown was for people who lived here or summered here or were spending the weekend here. The numbers had swollen, but what did it matter? If we were separated in the crowd, we knew our way around. Sydney could find her way home with one eye closed.

And Tripp... Well, he seemed to be doing a little better. Remembered what day it was and what we had planned and didn't suggest we go bungee jumping or deep-sea diving, thank God. Courtney had not brought the hoverboard he'd been so excited about because they don't let them on planes anymore—it was the first question Caroline had asked her as she helped her to her room. Not "Did you have a smooth flight?" or "Would you like to call your mother and tell her you're here?" I think if I hadn't been standing nearby, she might have gone through the child's luggage, aiming to confiscate anything that remotely looked like fun. I know she was furious that the child showed up, but really, why couldn't Sydney have a little friend along? How dull for a child to have only her parents, grandparents, and uncle for company! Finally, Tripp had done something that made a modicum of sense!

We stood on the lawn of our little cottage, waiting for Tom to finish in the bathroom, as he managed to sleep later than anyone despite being on the couch in the middle of everything. Eyes closed, mouth closed, one hand under his head like a little cherub. He had always looked so peaceful, so calm. Even as a little boy, getting a shot or falling off his bike. Never hysterical, like some little boys can be. I always thought he'd choose a profession that would make good use of that, a diplomat or surgeon, but when I told him those things, he'd just laugh.

Now he'd grown into a calm man with a job that didn't require the use of any of his gifts. The boys he went to school with were litigators and doctors and senators. I imagine their parents asking, "Whatever became of Tom Warner?" and being told he had the best job in the world. Drinking wine all day. The fathers would laugh, but the mothers would frown. They knew better.

Still, Tom had always had a nice relationship with his father, balancing Tripp's upbeat energy, and I didn't think twice when Tom bounded outside, hair damp from the shower, and announced that he and his dad were going to split off for a little bonding time. They'd watch a little Wimbledon, then look at yachts down at Straight Wharf, talk to the fishermen. I told him that sounded like an excellent idea, as if he'd thought of it himself, as if I didn't know it had been preordained. Even children who don't get along particularly well will conspire against you if given the chance. All mothers know this.

John said nothing. Didn't offer to go along with Tom, just followed us with his mouth shut. We walked into town the quickest and safest way, on the sidewalk, along Bathing Beach Road. It was crystal clear they were in cahoots. Caroline and I hardly needed any assistance with the girls. But the decree had been laid down.

I followed like a lemming. My own fault, in retrospect. After all, I was the one who asked them for help. And isn't it always your closest lieutenants who stage the coup?

Caroline

L ike a lot of truly beautiful people, my mother wasn't much of a shopper, because she didn't need to be. She had no use for embellishment. She had glossy hair and sparkling eyes—a cloak and two jewels. That's how she was raised, to let herself shine through. Still, she loved color and art and appreciated good design, and she approved of fresh air and exercise, so she enjoyed window-shopping tremendously. There were just enough art galleries and antique stores to pique her interest in town, and she lingered over the most tasteful displays, appreciated the lush arrangements of flower boxes, combinations that seemed to get more inventive every year. It was good to see her out, away from the houses, away from the specter of Bear Brownstein.

The girls were enchanted by all the people, particularly the teenagers a few years older, dressed in a style I can only describe as slutty mermaid. Flowing spaghetti straps, garlands of red stars in their hair. Like they were headed to Coachella and not trying to hitch a ride to Nobadeer Beach to drink some beer with older boys. According to John, that's what all the high school girls did on July 4—try to crash the college students' parties.

William, one of our neighbors who had survived raising three teenage daughters, had warned us about this. *Never let them go to Nobadeer Beach on Fourth of July. Never bring them to the island during*

Figawi Weekend in May. And never let them walk into town past nine o'clock in the summer. There was a special brand of trouble available in paradise, as evidenced by those attacks on the beach. Summer girls, island boys? I knew something about that. But far worse than people who were different were people who were just like us. I knew all this, and yet, it all still seemed far away. When other parents told us kids danced like porn stars at middle school dances, when other parents told us all the code words kids invented that mean *blow job*, we'd look at each other and think, *No, no, no, that wasn't Sydney.*

And then Courtney arrived, with her eye makeup and shorter shorts. I followed Sydney's gaze as she watched how Courtney reacted, how things dazzled her on the street. The clothing, the jewelry, the hair; it sparkled in front of the girls, made their shorts and tank tops and Converse look like artifacts from another civilization, and they knew it. Mesmerized not by an older boy but by something that could be far more dangerous. An older girl.

We divided just before we hit Main Street. We warned the girls to stay together, within my eye line, and that if anyone got lost, we should meet under the map of the world painted on the wall at Ralph Lauren.

Was it my imagination, or were there more police patrolling the street than usual? We saw several on bikes, a few on foot. Nantucket police tended to be young, fit, tan themselves. Like lifeguards with guns.

We squeezed past the long line outside the Fog Island Café, and then Tom and Dad turned left down the short, cobblestoned street between Lilly Pulitzer and the Club Car. They were heading toward Straight Wharf, entering the back way through Nantucket's version of an alley: a gravel drive with million-dollar boathouses that looked like a private driveway, until you crunched your way down to a wooden gate with a dot of a sign that read *Public way*. The most private kind of public.

We stood for a while with the girls, listening to the street guitarists play a cover of a song I didn't know. Courtney and Sydney knew every measure. They tapped their Converse, mouthed the words. The boys were an indeterminate age; they could have been sixteen or twenty-five, with their long, clean hair and soft, tanned skin. They sang in harmony, sang pretty well, truth be told. They finished the song, bowed slightly, and the whole block clapped. Sydney took out a one-dollar bill from her pocket and put it in one of their guitar cases.

"Thank you, darlin'," the guitarist said to her.

She blushed, Courtney giggled, and I took a deep breath. Damn it. My daughter was going to grow up. She was going to grow up and be beautiful, and there was no getting around it.

As we walked, I saw her drawn to a window outside Vis-A-Vis, a store that seemed far too old for her. Filmy red sundresses, ripped jeans, white camisoles with straps so thin, you could bite them in two. Clothes like a dam that couldn't hold. She seemed to be pondering whether she liked them or not, if they would look good on her.

"Ew," Courtney said, looking at the dress with distaste. "It's so...*long*."

"Yeah, totally," Sydney said, and my heart ached.

Don't be that girl! I wanted to say. But too late. Courtney led; Sydney followed. That's what came of having a hoverboard.

John walked along gamely, one of the few men looking into store windows. The benches up and down the street were filled with men checking their phones and drinking coffee while their wives shopped and their kids had their faces painted.

"Not as crowded this year," my mother remarked. "Dear God," she said after we passed a girl wearing a white slip dress and sunglasses. "If she's wearing that in July, what on earth will she wear in August?"

We usually made our way to the top of Main, went up toward the monuments, and sat down on the benches near Fair Street. Sydney had always called it Fairy Street, after a story I used to tell her about a prince and his princess who lived on Nantucket and used to ride their golden bikes down the street and look at all the house names—*Fair Thee Well, Fair Weather Friend*—and wonder what they'd name their house, and she said *Fairy Dust* and he said *Fair Enough.* At night, they'd go swim in the navy-blue darkness, with the fish glowing bioluminescent in circles around them. They'd climb into other people's boats in the harbor, dreaming about where they'd sail to. And the moment they stepped out of the water, the stars lit their path home.

Of course, I didn't tell her it was about me and Matt. I didn't tell her about him singing "Sweet Caroline" to me under the stars, or how we'd wade into the surf and fish for stripers in the moonlight, then cook them in a bonfire on the beach and still be home by eleven. But one time, John listened at the door as I told her the story, and something in his face told me that he knew. It didn't matter, but he knew.

When we passed Mitchell's bookstore, my mother turned to me.

"Oh, they have the new Nathaniel Philbrick. I have to get it for your father."

"Mom," I said, then paused. Her eyes stopped me like a cold, hard metal gate.

"He can still read, Caroline."

"Yes," I said. "Of course he can."

"We're going into the bookstore," I called to the girls. "Stay with Daddy."

John, about to sit on the bench, nodded, and so did Sydney, standing near him. Courtney was looking back toward the guitar players. Mother knew the woman working behind the counter and they chitchatted. I was reading the jacket copy of a book about Madeleine Albright when something made me turn and look out the store window. A dog's yelp, a child's squeal.

John was not seated at the bench anymore. I went outside and looked up and down the street. I saw a mother with triplets in identical blue dresses. I saw two of my mother's friends, Beryl and Joan, crossing the street. No John, no Sydney. Still, I wasn't concerned; they must be together, right?

I went outside, texted John, and the panic was just beginning to bubble in my throat.

"Where are the girls?" my mother asked.

"I don't know. I guess they're with John. We'd better head to the meeting spot."

People streamed out of the Ralph Lauren store, clutching bags, buying things they could buy anywhere but chose to buy here. We stood beneath the painted map of the world, in the way of everyone taking selfies, as if announcing ourselves, staking a claim.

And then my husband ran up—not from Main Street but from the other direction, the surf shop, where kids always gathered. His face was red and damp.

"What's happened?" I asked, grabbing his arm.

"They were standing right near the bookstore, petting a dog, and I got a text from Tom, and the next thing I knew, they were gone."

"A dog?"

"Well, a puppy. A yellow lab puppy with a red ban—"

"I don't need a description of the dog, John!"

"Well, if we find the dog, we might—"

"What about the dog's owner?"

"He was a guy. Maybe twenty-five—"

"Jesus Christ!" I started to pace. I looked up and down the street, turned in every direction. Of course they were safe. They weren't at the beach. They weren't in the moors. They were surrounded by families, by moms, by people who could help. By police. I repeated those things to myself quickly, but it didn't help. My heartbeat quickened. I felt something ancient and volcanic rise up in my body.

"I'm sure they're close, and they'll meet us here any minute," John said calmly.

"Yeah, unless the pedophile rapist asks if they want to see the other puppies in his van with the tinted fucking windows!"

"Caroline, don't—"

"If you tell me to calm down, I will scream bloody murder, John! You left my daughter with a man who had a puppy! How many red flags were flying over her head?"

"Now, Caro, come on. There are no pedophiles on Nantucket!" my mother proclaimed.

"You saw the posters! They're looking for someone!"

She breathed deeply. "He wasn't a pedophile."

"I suppose there are no thieves or arsonists or people capable of hate crimes either, right, Mother? Jesus, every subcontractor on this island drives a van!"

"Wait, did you say you got a text from Tom?" my mother asked.

"Yes," John said, but he said it too quietly, looked down at his shoes.

"Was something wrong with Tom?" my mother continued.

"Oh yes, let's not forget precious Tom! What missive was so fucking important from Tom that you took your eyes off your daughter? Buck a shuck? A new IPA on tap?"

He swallowed hard. "Actually," he said, "I didn't want to worry you yet, but—the girls aren't the only ones lost in the crowd today."

Tom

I t was terrible timing.

Not that my dad would slip away into the crowd the minute I turned my back, but that I would run into my sister before I found him. I would've rather run into an old girlfriend I'd dumped, a friend I owed money to, a professor who wondered if I had ever lived up to my potential. (No, Professor, no, I have not.)

I figured an old man in whale-patterned pants in a sea full of kids with squirt guns would not be that difficult to find. Two minutes, I thought, tops. But my sister's face, grim with fury, was a cinch to spot in a joyous crowd. It radiated heat. It singed. It stung.

We'd stopped at the piano bar at the Club Car, at Dad's request, since he loved to sing. That's where he and Mom had always had a drink before dinner in town, so I figured, what's the harm? It's a holiday. I hope to God when I'm Dad's age, no matter what my issues are, that I'm not denied a slab of beef, a tumbler of whiskey, a bowl of ice cream, and a place to sing at the top of my lungs. It's ridiculous what hard-asses my mother and sister have become. He's headed for lockup, for Christ's sake. Is there going to be a piano bar and Glenfiddich in assisted living? I fucking doubt it. So Caroline wanted my rationale, demanded my rationale, and there it is. I felt for the guy. He was moving to a place with bad food, no music, and no Scotch.

There were other men in there, refugees from the nonsense outside. Dad sat at the corner of the bar, closest to the front door, and that was my mistake.

At the end of a Billy Joel song, I walked three steps over and put a five-dollar bill in the tip jar. Three steps, five dollars. And my dad was gone, the door swinging on its hinges.

A woman at the cabstand told me he'd headed right, toward the top of Main Street, in a hurry. Remembered his whale-patterned pants. I was relieved that he hadn't headed toward Straight Wharf, toward the water, where a man taking off his shoes, boarding a boat, even jumping in the water to check something, wouldn't seem odd in the slightest.

"Do you want us to call the police?" the woman called out to me as I sprinted past.

"No!" I called out. Christ, that would be just what I needed—Billy Clayton. How many more police reports would it take until someone in my family was arrested for something? Heckling, arson, conspiracy, theft, drinking and singing with the elderly without a permit?

I headed up the cobblestone street, looking at a taco truck, a flower truck, a pickup full of CSA vegetables. Had he taken another truck? Would he try to find Sydney, his partner in crime? Would he head home?

I stood in the middle of Main Street, with the painted faces and balloons and guitars, looking in every direction for a man lost at sea. Did my father know his days were numbered? It was entirely possible, in that thin-walled house, that he had feigned sleep, heard our whispered plans. Or maybe, as an old man, you know it in your bones: *They're coming for you.*

I walked a half block toward the farmers market, scanning the crowd. I texted John, to give him a heads-up, enlist a little backup. Maybe he'd seen him. Maybe he could look for him in his spare time between holding his wife's purse and buying his daughter candy. I turned in circles, eyes open, debating my options, trying not to panic, when my sister's gaze laser-beamed onto mine. Too late. She saw me. I couldn't hear her above the crowd and the music, but I saw her lips move. *What the fuck!*

"I can't find Dad," I said quietly, evenly.

"I can't find Sydney," she replied.

Okay, Caroline, you win. She always won. I almost believed she had made it up, had urged her daughter to run away and hide just so she could have the upper hand.

"Is she with Courtney?"

"I don't know, Tom, since I can't currently see her!"

"I mean, Courtney's not here either? So they're together then, and—"

She held up her hand. "Stop talking," she said. "I don't need a man with no children to tell me about the buddy system and how she's old enough to take care of herself."

"Where's John?"

"We split up to look."

"Mom?"

"She went home."

I nodded. "Good," I said. "In case anyone is headed there."

My mother's point of view was always that nothing illegal ever happened on Nantucket except a bonfire. But she couldn't say those things to Caroline. Caroline didn't believe those things anymore, even if the world did.

"So you didn't call 911?"

"No, did you?"

"I think the Nantucket police are a little tired of hearing our name, don't you?"

We were standing there, squabbling, doing nothing to help the situation, when John walked up the small alley near Met on Main with the girls in tow.

"Sydney," Caroline said sternly, "I told you to stay with your father!"

"But Mom—"

"We thought you'd run off with the gypsies," I said, ruffling her hair. Keeping it light. But Caroline glared at me.

"We needed to get water for the puppy!"

"Where is this man with the puppy? Show me!"

"It wasn't a man. It was the boys from the band."

Sydney and Courtney bent over their phones, laughing.

"We took a Snapchat. It's so funny!"

Caroline spun in every direction around until she saw them. The boys from the band, now walking a tiny dog with a thick red rope. She started off, and John grabbed her arm.

"Honey," he said.

"Don't 'honey' me," she said, ripping her arm from his grasp.

I ran ahead and blocked her path. "Don't do this, Caroline. Don't embarrass your kid."

"What the hell do you know about raising a child, Tom? Get out of my fucking way!"

What did I know? Once upon a time, I'd been the guy with the puppy. I could get girls of any age to fawn over me, walking through a park with a dog.

"No," I said. "I won't let you do that to her." I grabbed her arms and crossed them, wrapping her up like a straitjacket.

She kicked her feet wildly, bruising my legs.

"Let me go!" Caroline screamed.

I carried her past the liquor store and deposited her outside the Starlight, a half block away from her family.

"Calm the fuck down," I said. "We need to find Dad."

"You lost him, you find him," she said, shoving me in the shoulder.

"Maybe he went back to the Club Car."

"Unbelievable. Can you not go one hour without a drink? You're drunk, aren't you? Jesus, Tom!"

"I am not drunk!"

"That's why you keep losing him. You've been drunk the whole time!"

John joined us while the girls held back, on their phones. Probably terrified to see Caroline raving like a loon.

"John, man," I said. "Do you think maybe Tripp headed home? If he knew no one was there?"

"What?" Caroline said. "Why would you think that?"

John and I exchanged a glance. I knew what that meant—I had to tell her.

"He seemed intent on going up to the widow's walk," I said. "He, uh, went up there alone."

"When?"

"A few nights ago." It seemed like an eternity to me now. "He was a little obsessed. I guess I could run back there, see if anyone saw him."

"Saw who?" Sydney asked, suddenly alert after focusing on her phone. She looked like she had just emerged from a swim and found strangers on the beach.

"Pop," I said.

"Oh, we saw him."

"What? Where?"

She pointed behind her. "He said he was going to go up to the church tower. He wanted us to come, but I told him we had to help the puppy. And then—"

"What, honey? What?"

"I was afraid to go, because of the van."

"Yes, honey, good. You did the right thing."

"But, Mom," she said quietly. "He tried to convince me. He said 'koala.'"

"Oh my God," Courtney said. "I cannot believe you still have a code word! Mine was 'unicorn.' Ha-ha, can you stand it?"

I didn't wait to hear the rest of it. I didn't walk. I ran up to the Congregational Church. Three blocks, four, uphill. A beautiful church, white, soaring. The lawn manicured. A picture postcard, most of the time. But not now. The tower was closed. The white church was wrapped in gray steel scaffolding.

And when I caught my father near the back of the property, looking up, trying to find a way to swing up his legs and climb, when I touched him on his arm and told him it was time to go home, he simply said, "I just wanted to see it all, Tommo. I wanted to see it all before it's gone."

Matt

It's fair to say I'm used to unusual requests. Impossible requests. Drunken requests. I've pretty much heard it all.

A wife who wanted me to fix her dishwasher "within the hour" because she was having a small dinner party and had no maid to wash the dishes. A man who wanted me to go through his septic system by hand to search for a ring, because tools might damage the gold. Those things are commonplace. Those things are any given Tuesday. I've learned how to say no a thousand different ways and learned to say yes in a way that means *Okay, but never ask me to do this again.*

But Alice's request was a first: she wanted to hire a bodyguard for her husband. Just to get them through the week. I told her I'd come over to discuss it. A delay tactic, for sure. But I needed time—not to decide, not to find just the right person, but to craft, carefully, what I needed to say. I did not go over there to see her daughter.

But how can you keep anything from Caroline? I asked Alice to meet me at their house, since I needed to check on it anyway. Make sure the tarps were secure in the front, since the sod hadn't come in yet. Make sure there was no new graffiti or broken windows or any other signs of mischief. The things you might do in the off-season.

When she was five minutes late, then ten, I started walking over to the cottage.

No sign of Alice as I approached. Car gone. Maybe she'd changed her mind? Then the door banged open, and out came Caroline.

"I hope to God you ignored her," she said.

"What?"

"When she asked you for security detail," she said, laughing. "Jesus. What was she thinking, that you could just fly over some bouncers from the Cape?"

"You think it's funny?"

She turned to me, her eyes suddenly cold. I'd forgotten how quickly they could turn dark.

"Well," she said with a sigh, "since you're alone, I'm going to assume you'll tell her you couldn't find anyone."

"Caroline," I said calmly, "I can find anything my clients ask for, if the price is right, and if I want to."

"Yet here you are. Solo."

"Yes."

"Here to do what, exactly?"

"Here to tell your mother to take your father home."

"This is his home. Nantucket is as much his home as it is yours."

I opened my mouth, then closed it. She still had the power to wound me. To wound anyone. Some people are born with hard edges and are softened over time, tumbled down, eroded. And others always hit rock, not rolling wave, not foam; they just become sharpened, flintier.

"It's the right thing to do."

"Jesus, Matt, what makes you so fucking smart? That you know all the answers all the time?"

I turned to leave. "Tell your mom to take him home, Caroline. Where it's safe. Before your luck runs out."

I was around the corner before I heard her following me. The sound of leather flip-flops flying across macadam—that was the sound of summer, more than anything else. Flip-flops and screen doors. The mid-island symphony.

She followed me, and I waited to hear it, ringing out: That Tripp had a right to be here! That she had a right to have a vacation too! But it didn't come. Her feet followed me, but not her voice. Maybe she hoped I'd look back, change my mind, offer something up. But I didn't. And neither did she.

I held my ground, and she held hers, all the way to my truck, all the way to her house. When I pulled away, I didn't see her in my rearview mirror. I looked for her, for her faded red T-shirt and her blue jean shorts and her always-tanned legs. I was wired to look for her everywhere.

But this time, I don't know where she went.

Maggie Sue

Other housecleaners think there should be a special place in hell reserved for people who ask you to come on the Fourth of July in the hour and a half space between when the caterer leaves and their guests arrive. Not me. But there should be a special place reserved at the ATM for people who are paid triple time to do it, so you can deposit their check before they come to their senses.

Old Lady Grinstaff would never have done such a thing, but her daughter-in-law does things a little differently, and that's why I found myself cleaning at 7:30 p.m. before her guests arrived for fireworks and desserts. They had another party in a few days, part of the block association, and I was scheduled for that one too, a fancy one. But this was supposed to be "casual."

How do you casually clean? The gardener raked seaweed from the beach. The caterer answered the request for "luxury but not fancy" with brownies. Me, I organized. I lit the sea salt candles. I arranged red linen cocktail napkins around the chilled rosé and champagne. I plumped their down sofa cushions so people could put their sandy asses on them after watching fireworks on the narrow strip of beach.

Anyway, that's why I happened to be there, right on the harbor, catty-corner across the street from the Warners'. And why, as I walked to my car in the opposite direction from everyone who was walking down to watch fireworks, I heard them, the whole family, down there on the public way.

Was I sure it was their voices and not someone else's? I could just hear Billy Clayton asking me that, phrasing the same question three different ways, as if that would trip me up. As if a cleaning woman was only capable of seeing things. You forget all the time I spend listening. The sounds of a house, of a family, when you are just a ghost in the next room. I knew their voices by heart. The force of Alice's, the flat monotone of Tom's, the throaty catch of Caroline's. The angrier she got, the more she put behind it, the more it broke apart in the air. Was that what happened that night when she was young—the harder she tried to scream, it just tore up into nothing?

Her brother wanted to go to Jetties. She said, "Fine, you guys go then. I'll watch Dad."

I thought nothing of it. I walked to my car and drove away. I was just past the Dreamland Theater when I heard the first booms of the fireworks. And I didn't hear anything else until morning.

Tom

Me and Caroline fighting. I don't remember if it was the music of our childhood, but it sure as shit was the symphony of our adulthood. She chose to fight, picked at ordinary things until they burned. She said I threw things in her face. Flaunted them. Forced her hand.

Sometimes we were two dogs who didn't know how to let go of a rope, sometimes two kids throwing temper tantrums at the same time. Always, though, there was equivalence. If not equal amounts of pain, there were equal amounts of blame.

I'm trying to think, now, of all the times our family holidays were ruined and whether it was always my fault. That's part of the fabric of life, right? Ruined holidays? Everybody has them. You repeat the stories at anniversaries, weddings, and yes, funerals. These things happen, tragic at the time, but then they soften, form into funny stories. There was a Christmas Eve standing rib roast, demolished by Aunt Laila's black lab when she turned her back. I still remember all of us looking at the empty silver platter as if it were an archaeological dig, wondering where the bones had gone.

But now, that Fourth of July has made mincemeat of all other holiday memories; we've taken the ultimate family bonding experience and ruined it forever. We'll never laugh about it or retell it. And somehow, of course, it was all my fault. Well played.

It started off around the idea of a clambake. He'd brought it up a few days before, and I asked my mother if we could make it happen. She had more chowder in the freezer; I'd seen it when I'd gone in for the vodka bottle. That was her secret, all these years; make it when no one was watching, then freeze it. And you'd always have "fresh" chowder.

Mom and Caroline thought a bonfire was too dangerous in Dad's current state, and I suppose they were right. At the rate he was going, he might try to teach the girls to walk on hot coals. But a sunset picnic would be a suitable stand-in, and we'd do it across the street, on the smaller spit of beach, where there'd be fewer people. We spread the plaid blankets, anchored the area with metal lanterns. Mom had a big insulated container of chowder, just as he'd asked for, and Caroline had made a batch of curried mussels with spinach and potatoes. We ate out of tin bowls, splatter-painted blue and white, the same ones we'd had when I was a kid. The feel of the metal lip when I slurped the last dregs of chowder was as familiar to me as my own razor or toothbrush or anything I'd ever owned.

The boats in the harbor were strung with lights, and the wind was calm. My father seemed tranquil for the first time all week; for once, he didn't want any more than what was in front of him. He didn't ask why we didn't go out in our boat, which bobbed within sight, or why ours wasn't strung with holiday lights. (My mother found this kind of display horrifying.) No more suggesting outrageous activities, no more animated outbursts. He ate his chowder; he squeezed my mother's hand. He looped an arm over my shoulder.

But the girls were restless. They picked at their mussels, dipping the bread in the broth but eating little else. They walked up and down the narrow beach several times, looking not for beach glass or shells but for something indefinable, something you couldn't name when you were an adolescent.

"Let's go down to Jetties," I said.

"To the bar?" Caroline said.

"No, to the beach."

"To the beach with a bar."

"That's not—"

"You can see the fireworks just as easily from here."

"But it's bigger and more…exciting there. For the kids."

"It's the same fireworks whether you're there or here!"

"But there are more people. Maybe more young people."

John said the next thing. "Tom and I could take the girls down there, and—"

"And what? Maybe let them get lost again? Leave them so they can walk home in the dark with a rapist on the loose?"

"Caroline, no. Of course not."

She stood there a few seconds. I didn't know what was going through her mind, only that something was. What I wouldn't give to see the instant replay, the tape she ran, the game plan she formed. How my sister's mind worked was a mystery to all of us.

"Fine, you guys go then. I'll watch Dad."

I thought it was decent of her to offer to go with Dad to give the rest of us a break. "It was my turn," she said afterward. Did I think twice about this? No, not really. She was the strongest person we all knew.

I was the first person to recognize something had happened. The sky in front of us was an explosion of beauty—blues flowering out of reds, people's heads tilted up, hopeful, happy. The booms and squeals of the fireworks, the oohs and aahs of the crowd. Then, the sound of something different raining down behind us. Not the bright sparkling pop and showering sparks. No. A terrible cracking, closer to lightning than fireworks, then a scream. Whose, I didn't know. I turned first. I saw the kind of dust I remembered from watching a demolition.

The girls watched the finale over their shoulders as we pulled them toward the street. The sirens started then, and John broke into a run. Not because of what he knew, but because of what he didn't know. He didn't know where Caroline was.

"Take the girls to the cottage," he screamed at Alice. "Go with your grandmother, Sydney. Do you hear me? Go straight to the cottage."

We turned the other way, toward the old house. I saw something on the ground: litter, trash. I smelled something burning in the air. Fireworks, flesh. I didn't know then, and I don't know now.

And then there was Caroline, finally, standing in the street. Her tears glistening and huge, not falling, but there. Very definitely there, poised at the top of her cheekbones.

"He got away from me," she said.

Later, I asked John if Caroline had been crying or sweating.

"Crying," he said.

"Are you sure?"

"They looked like tears. Real tears."

"I'm sure they did," I replied.

And I wondered if you could test the difference. If you could collect the drops and put them under a microscope, ignore the salty sameness, and know, for certain, what they were.

Matt

I slanders feel about the Fourth of July the way bartenders feel about New Year's Eve. Amateur hour. Crazy town. Firecrackers, bottle rockets, Roman candles, all of it—it's just halfway, just a stand-in. Men hide behind them as if they're displaying some kind of courage. Men who don't know how to do anything but light a match.

I live in fear of one of my clients' kids doing something idiotic on the Fourth. To themselves or to the property. But I never thought it would be the Warners. Never.

I had been up on the Cliff, fixing a porch light, when I heard the ambulance. Assumed it was for Tripp, since they hadn't listened to me. I knew better than to go there, to risk Caroline's wrath once again. How angry would she be that I'd been right about her father? Then I heard someone on the street say that a house had collapsed, that there had been an accident, and I ran to my car.

I parked a few houses away and walked up the street, outside the perimeter of the crime tape, and felt sick to my stomach. Their house. *My house.* The plinths of wood all over the lawn, sharp as toothpicks but enormous, like something out of a bad dream. It smelled like the shop at a lumberyard. The protest of wood, the scream of metal.

The roofing tiles had soared through the air and landed, bent, broken. They'd been new, those tiles. Hadn't seen any wind, snow, bird shit yet. And the wetness, on the old tarp, the grass. Even in the dark, I knew it was blood as much as dew. Whoever was up there had to have hit every surface, every sharp edge possible on the way down.

Billy Clayton moved around with three others, working. All the spectators gone; the family too. Who had been up there? Tripp? Or the whole family? Was that it, the weight of the whole family? Every year when I jumped up and down on the widow's walk, the porches, testing for the soft parts. When I looked at the framing, checked for weakened wood. Could it not hold their weight?

I stood on the corner lot next door, behind a hedge, watching, hidden. I wanted to ask but knew I could be blamed. Better not to make myself known.

He was down on one knee, circling his flashlight around, over and over. Why was he looking on the ground and not on the roof? Anyone could do the quick calculations in their head. Distance. Height. Weight. Angle. Pitch. Either the widow's walk came down on its own—rotting wood, built too high, too much weight—or someone took it down. So why were these guys looking at the ground?

The blue hydrangeas ringing the house dripped with dew. Not great for collecting footprints or fingerprints. Two of the bushes were smashed, branches broken, flowers dangling at odd angles, petals littering the grass. Billy reached inside the base, spread them apart, peering at the sandy ground.

He waved his team over, and they took photos. Of a footprint? Of an impression?

"Dented footing," he said, and I heard him loud and clear.

How many men on this island, walking by, listening in, would know what that meant? I knew.

And I could see it now, hanging in the Warners' basement on a hook, the ladder with one dented foot. The ladder that wobbled.

The ladder I never used, but they did. Tripp Warner was too cheap to replace it. It worked just fine, he always said. You just had to be careful.

FROM THE DESK OF LIEUTENANT
BILLY CLAYTON

Investigation of Tripp Warner Death
Notes from Brownstein Interview, July 5, 2017,
    8:00 a.m.
Suspect said he'd been inside all night reading
No witnesses to corroborate
Thought ambulance lights were fireworks
Ate dinner at Yoshi's, paid cash; Yoshi confirms
Fresh footprints between hedge and Hulbert Ave
Insists the Warners are out to get him, not the
    other way around
Claims he owns no tools or ladder
Brief tour of house seems to support this; suspect
    asked for search warrant
When asked what book he was reading all night,
    grabbed one off shelf
Book spine cracked as if new

Matt

News travels faster on an island than other places. Fewer people, less to do, everyone knows everyone. Sometimes it's silly to even call it news; it's just information.

So I was surprised, when I came back the next morning to assess the repairs, that the neighbors hadn't gotten the memo that they were staying elsewhere. Two flower arrangements and three casserole dishes took up a good bit of real estate on the porch.

I loaded the dishes into my truck; they were still warm. *Good*, I thought. *Nothing has spoiled.* A few of the Warners' old friends still behaving like people do.

When I brought them to the cottage, no one was there, even the girls. I put everything in the kitchen, left a note, and when I walked outside, Billy Clayton was waiting in his car. Said he needed to talk to me.

FROM THE DESK OF LIEUTENANT
BILLY CLAYTON

Investigation of Tripp Warner Death

Notes from Matt Whitaker interview, July 5, 2017,
    9:00 a.m.

Confirmed he was still the caretaker and had key

Said the Warners no longer performed own upkeep
    or repairs

Couldn't remember the last time he'd been at the
    house

Didn't know if widow's walk had ever been inspected

Said he usually used his own tools and equipment

Allowed me to look in his truck and examine
    ladders

When asked who else had access to his house keys,
    he said his wife

Insisted wife did not know he'd been romantically
    involved with Caroline Warner

Maggie Sue

I guess they forgot I was coming.

People get caught up in their out-of-town guests, their fishing trips and beach hauls, their deliveries, their arrivals, the comings and goings that matter most, and are shocked when I show up at the door. At my regular, appointed time, like clockwork. I'm Cinderella, there to make their world sparkle and shine, and they look at me like I'm a dental hygienist come to scrape their teeth.

I was relieved, as I pulled my car onto the grass spit separating their house from the street, that the outside was cleaned up already. The grass torn up and rototilled. A small Dumpster in the driveway, and I didn't want to look, didn't want to think what might be inside. I expected maybe crime tape circling the house, or some sort of rope, but there was nothing. Oh, I don't know what I expected. This was a new one.

Given what had happened, I called ahead to make sure they still wanted me there, that the house still needed to be cleaned, and Alice wasn't there when I called, but Tom said yes, absolutely, that it still had to be cleaned before they left the next day. He said no one would be there, that they were all staying elsewhere.

But I could tell from the look of shock on his sister's face when she opened the porch door that he hadn't mentioned this set of facts to her.

"I'm very sorry about your loss," I said.

"Thank you, but—"

"I spoke to your brother. He told me to come today and give it a once-over."

"A once-over?"

I blinked. I wasn't sure if that was exactly the term he used, but that was the gist of it. I felt my face start to redden, my words tangled on my tongue. How was it that girls like Caroline had always been so certain of everything that they made me feel uncertain?

"Yes," I said, because I couldn't think of anything else to say that wouldn't come out wrong.

I heard something in the kitchen then, and I saw that she wasn't alone. Billy Clayton clearing his throat, like a warning.

"Did he already pay you?"

"I'm paid in advance at the beginning of the seas—"

"Never mind," she said. "Just…do what you need to do."

Such a strange way to put it. As if I was driven by some compulsion to clean. I'd be happy to take the money and do nothing for it. I wasn't an idiot. I didn't live to wipe up their crumbs. And now, the house—was it haunted? Tainted? The air inside felt sealed up already. Cold. The summer had barely begun, and it felt like it was gone already.

I went upstairs. The second and third floors weren't really dirty. Some sticky mouthwash rings in the bathrooms. Some dust on the bedside tables. I knew if there was any real work to be done, it would be in the kitchen. But that's where the two of them were. I heard the low thrum of their voices, drawers opening, kettle whistling, then the familiar squeak of the old basement door. Not footsteps going down; just the door opening and then closing. Didn't come upstairs and look either. Guess he didn't have a warrant yet.

Once I asked Matt Whitaker about that door, why he hadn't oiled it, tightened it. Everything else, every spidery trail of mold on the wall, every loose floorboard, every nick of paint, was always touched up, tended. But not the door. He had smiled, like he was remembering something, and said the family didn't want to waste money on anything in the basement. *Yeah, right,* I wanted to say. Like he hadn't wiped down and organized everything down there already, on his own dime.

I took my time upstairs, giving them ample opportunity to finish up and leave. I wiped down the banister, the floorboards. I dusted picture frames, which I almost never do. At last, I heard the thump of the screen door, flip-flops on the porch steps.

"Finally," I muttered and carried the vacuum cleaner down the steps, not bothering to wind the cord, letting it snake behind me. Why rich people never had two or three vacuum cleaners, one for each floor, I would never know. Mysteries of the universe. Then it hit me: one set of footsteps leaving. Not two.

He sat at the kitchen table with a glass of water, paper, pen. Like an interrogation room.

"I gotta clean in here," I said dumbly. The things that come outta my mouth sometimes.

"It's not dirty."

"Maybe not to your eye."

He laughed, and I suppose I got his point. Who was more observant on this island than Billy Clayton?

"Were you cleaning here yesterday?"

"I'm here today, so no."

"Don't some people need you two days in a row?"

"Not the Warners."

"Ever?"

"Ever. Not that it should matter to you."

Sometimes I felt his power, just watching him drive around town, his window always down in case he missed something. Some sound that he might need to recall later. It wasn't fair, the things he felt he had every right to know, on his way to learning other things. He didn't need to know everything; he just liked to.

"You clean at the Brownsteins' yesterday?"

"No."

"Really?"

"Really."

"So you weren't at the Brownsteins' and weren't at the Warners', but your car was, more or less."

"You following me, Billy?"

"Maybe."

"I was cleaning at the Grinstaffs. Hard to park because of the fireworks. So I parked over here."

"When did you leave?"

"Just after dark."

"And you didn't come here."

"No. Do I have to say it louder for you to hear it?"

"And you didn't go to the Brownsteins'?"

"No, I just told you that, Billy!" My mother would have told him to clean his ears, but I thought that was a bit too intimate to say, even to someone I'd known since he was in a wading pool.

"You can see the house from where your car was parked. Both of them."

"Yeah, so?"

"So, did you see anything?"

"No."

"Didn't see anyone outside or cutting through the lawn between the Brownsteins' or—"

"You don't really think he did this?"

"Did what?"

"Chopped down the widow's walk?"

"Is that what you think happened?"

"Jesus, Billy, I don't know. Chopped, jerry-rigged, exploded, I don't know."

"Sounds like maybe you do."

"I don't."

"But whatever it is, you don't think Bear Brownstein did it."

"No."

"Because you're fond of him."

"No," I said hotly, my face turning red again.

What was it about Bear Brownstein? Well, we were both straight shooters. We understood each other. But what does that even mean to a man like Billy? That's not a fact; that's a feeling, like mist.

"Then why?"

"Because he's afraid of heights," I blurted out.

He hesitated. I knew the information was useful and unexpected. He was probably kicking himself for not noticing this, for not finding this out himself.

"How do you know that?"

"He told me."

"He told you? You two just sit around talking about your fears and foibles?"

"Christ on a cracker, Billy, why you gotta twist every little damned thing?"

"Twist it back then. Illuminate me."

"He asked me to go up on his library ladder and get him a book. Said he got all wobbly up high."

"Wobbly?"

"Yeah. So I climb up, and I'm rolling the ladder across, and I said, 'This one? Is this the book?' And when I looked down, he looked pale, just from watching me, just from tilting his head up."

He took a deep sigh. He'd seen the ladder of course. He'd seen all the books. You couldn't miss it when you stepped inside.

"Why would a man who was afraid of heights have that in his house?"

"I'm afraid of getting burned, but I still got an oven."

He breathed in deeply, tapped his pencil. He took a long swallow from the water glass.

"You through with that?" I asked, reaching for it. "Because I got dishes to do. And don't you have a rapist to catch? Don't you have better things to do than bother me?"

He handed it to me, stood up, put the pencil behind his ear. A golf pencil, I saw now.

"He's your employer, I get that. He tips you at the end of the season, he gives you his old outdoor furniture that cost more than your indoor furniture, he—"

"No, he doesn't," I said hotly. "Who told you that?"

"I'm speaking generally. I'm speaking symbolically, metaphorically."

"You don't know a thing."

"My point is, someone is nice to you, generous, makes you like them. And when you like someone, you tend to see things a certain way, isn't that right?"

I closed my eyes. People ask me sometimes, "Don't you ever get sick of living on an island? Don't you ever want to just drive off, and you can't?" And this is one of those moments. Sometimes you do, yeah. But it's not the island that does it; it's the people you can't escape. People who come here and just stick. Forever.

"Billy, that was a long time ago. I thought I did see him at Stubby's. It was dark, and I was a k—"

"Right. We were kids. Can't be held responsible for anything you do as a kid, can you?"

"No. No, you really can't."

Here was where our beliefs went in different directions. He was a law-and-order, charge-'em-as-adults kinda guy, and I was a he's-only-a-kid kinda gal. Both sides always believe they're right, and never the twain shall meet.

I filled the bucket with soapy water, turned my back on him. He walked across the kitchen and stopped.

"Must have hurt that you weren't invited to that slumber party," he said. "But then Caroline was just a kid, right?"

"You got any more questions for me, Billy? Or you just want to tease me about being unpopular when I was twelve?"

Caroline and Pippa, running up the beach together in their Speedos, ponytails flying. Girls like that made the most ordinary things look beautiful. Me with my unruly hair and skinned knees. I didn't belong with them, and we all knew it.

He hadn't asked if I'd heard anything, smelled anything, felt anything. Just what I'd seen. And that was his mistake. Whether it mattered or not, those moments July 4, I'd heard what I heard, and I didn't tell him because he didn't ask me directly and because I didn't really like him. Simple as that. Had nothing to do with her.

"I'm not teasing you," he said. "I'm dead serious. You hated her."

"I did not."

"You probably wished she'd tumbled off the walk, not her dad."

"Well, Billy, as long as we're having such a serious chat about our youth, one person I sure as hell didn't see at Stubby's that night Caroline got hurt was you. You and Connor Grinstaff used to hang out, but did anyone ask the cop's son about his whereabouts? Huh? Or did your daddy protect you like Connor's daddy did?"

His face burned, but I didn't care. He was taking advantage of me being in other people's homes. Like he had as much right to be there as I did, but he didn't.

"So you didn't see anything here on the Fourth?"

"Nope."

And because he didn't ask me if I heard anything, or smelled anything, or sensed anything, that's all I said. Asked and answered.

"One more question," he said. "You ever use the ladder when you clean? Get those cobwebs out of the corners?"

Everything sloshed as I pulled the bucket out of the sink. The plastic lip was cracked. The sink wasn't deep enough. The water was turned down too cool. It didn't really matter what Billy Clayton said or didn't say; it didn't matter what happened thirty years ago. Nothing we were talking about would change the cold, hard truth.

Because the truth is it didn't matter how carefully Matt Whitaker looked after it; nothing was ever right about that house, not level or true.

"Get out of this house, Billy."

"It's not yours."

"It is today."

Alice

One of my only concessions to my dotage is showering inside, not outside. No one needs to see an old woman in a towel walking around. No one wants to peek innocently out a third-floor window and get a glimpse of my gray head under a shower. No. Inside it is, in my own bathroom, in the shower or tub or whatever I choose. Started it the year I turned sixty and probably should have begun sooner. Bathing behind a closed door was sometimes the only time I was ever alone in the big house. I confess I used to look forward to my chores, because it gave me full rein while they were all off gallivanting. A big home calls out to guests, whether you intend it to or not. Of course, that's what my father always envisioned, and I carry that forward. Room for guests, always. Still, I secretly longed for it empty. Maybe it's not that secret anymore. Caroline always looks like she knows what everyone is thinking, even me.

The cottage is built better, solid, winterized. Can't even hear when the wind blows offshore. But even in the large bathroom, still, I can hear them outside the door: Tom, John—a deep voice he has, it carries more than the others—the squeals of Sydney with her little friend. Things going on without Tripp, things that are the same. Smaller now, in this smaller space. Fitting, perhaps, I think. Fitting.

In my bedroom—*mine, not ours*; I must practice that—a small vanity tucked up under an eave. I comb my hair, swipe on a bit of lipstick, a few modest passes of shadow, eyelashes curled. Concessions to the inevitable.

An old white dress, a new blue wrap, legs tan as a lizard, as they always are, but I don't look too worse for wear, I think, as I descend the stairs.

"Where are you going?" Caroline asked. They were all in the small kitchen. John slicing cucumbers, carrots. Neighbors' casseroles warming in the oven. I smelled curry, garlic, things Tripp had never liked. Moving on, all of us, already.

"To the party," I said.

"What...party?"

"The block party."

They looked at each other. Or I should say Caroline looked at Tom, and Tom looked at his feet, then John looked at Caroline. A round-robin, could have been like a tennis match. Ping, pong.

"What block party?"

"The progressive block party."

"You didn't mention this, Mom. I—"

"Well, you weren't invited. It's the homeowner's association, you see, and—"

"Mom," Tom started to say, "don't you think that maybe—"

"Maybe what, Tom?"

"That you should skip the party?"

"But we go every year!"

Surely my children remembered this!

"Mom, this year, maybe—"

"Because that man tore down half my house? I should hang my head in shame in front of the homeowner's association, because my home is damaged? I assure you, they'll side with me. I'll get full support. Maybe find a good lawyer to help."

"No, Mom, because of Dad." Caroline said *Dad* in such a way, so hard and long, that it almost sounded like dead. Did she intend that?

"Your father RSVP'd yes to that party, Caroline. He would want me to honor that."

Again, with the looks. As if I wouldn't notice. As if I wasn't standing right there.

"I think, under the circumstances, you'd be forgiven for being a no-show, don't you? I mean, you're grieving."

The kitchen, so small, much smaller than ours. The living room, tiny. The heat of their bodies, the oven, the smell of their foreign foods.

"Your father would not want me to grieve. Not for one second. If you need me," I said, "I'll be at the Grinstaffs'."

I threw that name out before I thought of it, and I confess, I regretted it a bit when I saw her face.

Here's how it had always worked: hors d'oeuvres at the first house, buffet dinner at the second, dessert at the third. It was always houses between Jetties and Brant Point. Members rotated hosting duties over the years. Tripp and I had only hosted twice. People rode bikes with lights; neighbors walked in formation. How many times he and I had walked, arm in arm, the smell of warm rolls and bubbling chowder in the air as we made our way up the street.

But this year, walking alone, I saw a long line of cars. When I got closer, I saw that they had an attendant. Valet parking, with tipping, at a party! And who needed to drive when they lived around the corner?

I walked up the circular driveway, crunching my way across the shells, shaking my head at the man who opened the door in a waiter's uniform. How many more employees would I encounter before I met the host and hostess?

I took a glass of champagne off a tray, wishing I'd called Beryl or Joan so we could arrive together. Everywhere I looked, there were young women dressed in high-heeled espadrilles. High heels at the beach! Who were these people? A few polite conversations led me to the belief that the Grinstaffs had invited a great many people beyond the local homeowners. There were people there from Madaket,

'Sconset, Wauwinet. Another tradition, out the window. I grabbed a shrimp skewer from a tray and nibbled it, thinking of Tripp. How he had loved shrimp. This one was chewy, overcooked.

Finally, a blond woman Caroline's age came up and introduced herself as Teddy Grinstaff. When I told her my name, she took a step back.

"From across the street?"

"Yes, of course."

"I'm sorry. I didn't expect you."

"Well, you invited me."

"Yes, but—"

"Of course, it appears you invited the entire island."

Her face clouded. "We try to be inclusive."

"Is Kit here?"

"Who?"

"Your…mother-in-law?"

"Oh, Katherine died last year."

I blinked. No one had told me. There'd been no obituary in the Nantucket paper.

"What a shame," I said. "So you buried her nickname with her, did you?"

"Will you excuse me?" she said, her eyes fixed on something overhead.

I found Beryl, at last, on the porch. She wasn't surprised to see me, not in the slightest. She said it was good that I was getting out. That I was carrying on. Life is for the living. I would accept all drinks, all skewers, and all condolences.

"They redecorated but haven't changed much at all, have they?" Beryl said as we looked inside from the deck. Behind the glass, the same long living room, the same placement of a game table and a telescope. Plusher sofas, carpet, sconces, yes, but the basics remained. "But the food is awful."

"Well," I said, "she may have won her divorce case, but that dreadful woman spent all her money on waiters."

"Yes," she agreed. "As if people don't have the strength to pick up their own hors d'oeuvres. And I heard they catered s'mores on the Fourth."

"Did they hire whittlers to carve out sticks for the marshmallows?"

We shared a laugh, skipped the food, and walked down to the next house on Brant Point, to the Marshalls', who had a sensible vat of fish stew bubbling, and where Karen Marshall was wearing an apron and wielding her own ladle, and who told me she was glad, so glad that I was there, that Tripp would have wanted me to come.

Of course he would.

But part of me wanted to tell her, tell someone, the awful truth. That Tripp also wanted me to kiteboard and jump out of a plane and ride a glittering, flashing skateboard from wherever we were to the next place. He was filled with want; for a man who appeared content, he simply wanted, far too much.

Caroline

I f Mom could take a night out yesterday, you can have one today," Tom said.

Out of the corner of my eye, I caught John shaking his head at Tom. *Don't go there. Wrong logic. Try again.*

"So you're saying I'm like Mom."

"He wasn't saying that," John said.

They were unlikely to win this argument now. I'd actually been considering my husband's offer until my brother jumped in and ruined things, as he often did.

"No, I wasn't," Tom continued. "I was saying you should become more like Mom."

John groaned. I kept my mouth closed and waited for them to pivot, try again. John was nothing if not persistent and determined in his own calm way.

"I mean, if a widow can allow herself pleasure, why not you? Why not try to salvage this vacation in a way that at least Dad would approve of?"

"Maybe we should go hoverboarding."

"Also, free babysitting," John said.

"Oh, they're old enough to take care of themselves," Tom said.

"They are not," I snapped.

I sighed. It had been a long time since John and I had gone out alone. Too much business travel for him. Too many early mornings on the river for me. Too much of Sydney's math homework to help with for us both. Some days, I thought I was still tired from giving birth twelve years ago, that I'd never caught up.

"How about we take out the boat?" John said. "Maybe go over to Wauwinet. I always think of your dad when we're on the boat."

"I think Pop would like that," Tom said.

I sniffed back the tears that were threatening at the corner of each eye. I knew they both meant well, but they had no idea what they were doing. None of their logic would make me feel better. But sitting around filled with regret and sadness and grief while we waited to change our ferry reservations wasn't doing me any good either. Listening to my mother scrub pans and wipe down cabinets in a house we didn't own and weren't paying for was making me jump out of my skin. I felt like I was just taunting Billy Clayton by waiting around. How long before he found me, grilled me again? How long before the search warrant arrived?

Wind in my hair. Salt spray across my cheeks. He couldn't find me on the water.

"Okay," I said. "You win."

We left Sydney and Courtney at the kitchen table, making cookies while my mother ordered them a pizza. Cookies and pizza. The only things girls and adolescents had in common.

Tom's only plan was to watch a baseball game and eat any cookies they deigned to give him. John and I walked the long way, up Beach Street to Easton, down to Brant Point, then over on the beach to our mooring, just so we could avoid going past the house. We waded out. John started up the boat, and I wiped down the wooden surfaces. It was impossible to keep a beautiful boat clean, but that didn't stop us from trying, from always dipping the sand off our feet, rinsing off, trying not to spill anything sticky.

As we headed slowly through the harbor, around the Point, I remembered how much my brother and father hated the imposed speed limits. How I thought of it as warming up, a respite, and they thought of it as holding themselves back.

John drove the boat even more carefully than I would, but I didn't mind. It was nice to appreciate the brisk air after a day full of hot tears. When we pulled up at the dock, the *Wauwinet Lady*, the boat the hotel used to ferry customers, was well behind us, and we tied up, grateful that we would get a drink and an Adirondack chair on the lawn before the crowd arrived to watch the sunset. We ordered scallops and mushroom pâté and two gin and tonics and balanced the small plates on the flat arms of the chairs looking out to sea. And then John started talking as the colors slowly seeped across the sky. Not about my family, not about my dad, but about vacations and places he'd like to go, things he'd like Sydney to see. Not overtly saying *Let's make new memories; let's start over fresh*, but it could be interpreted that way. And that was okay. I let him dream out loud, I added a few ideas of my own—Chautauqua, Penobscot, Vancouver—and then we settled in for the first part of the pink-and-orange light show. When the sun breached the horizon of the water, we headed back to the boat, to let the last glimmers of light guide us home.

This was my favorite part, not leaving but coming home. When navy blue started to take over the pastel sky, preparing for stars, moon. The in-between, not still day and not yet night.

As we rounded the jut that held Brant Point Lighthouse, a fire flickered on the beach. It illuminated a man, a guitar, a small group sitting and standing around him. A flash of beer cans, a silver zipper on a hoodie, glinted like fireflies.

"Remember those days?" John asked, and I smiled. I did and I didn't. So much beauty had been painted over with pain. Yes and no. As we passed them, a girl stood by the edge of the fire. The orange light shimmered across her, illuminating her hips as she danced. A strip of sequins at the bottom of a too-short shirt.

"John," I said, grabbing his arm. "That's Sydney!"

"What?"

"At the bonfire."

"What? That's crazy. How can you—"

"Her shirt! I saw her shirt!"

"Honey, there are probably a million kids with the same sh—"

"John, stop!"

He idled the engine. I rolled up my white jeans, kicked off my sandals, and dove into water that would have been too shallow if we'd been a foot closer. I knew those waters—the depth, the outcroppings—like I knew the floorplan of my own home. Like I knew the posture and outline of my own daughter.

When I walked onto the beach, dripping, furious, I'm sure I looked like a creature, a monster from the sea. The look on my daughter's face certainly would lead you to believe that.

She turned and ran when she saw me, grabbing Courtney by the wrist, sand spitting at her heels.

The music stopped, and all I heard was the sound of my clothes dripping onto the shallows of the low tide. I turned, wordlessly, and swam back to the boat.

Alice

Of course Tom didn't hear the girls leave. He didn't hear the announcer of the Red Sox game either as he fell asleep watching it. He'd been up all night the evening before, out on the lawn with his bourbon or what-not, watching the stars. Communing with his father, I suppose. Those two were the only successful relationship left in the family, I'd say.

I didn't sleep well either, truth be told. There was a tsunami of a to-do list awaiting me. So many people to call, so many tasks to perform. I was relieved we weren't in our house, in our own beds; it likely would have felt very empty without Tripp there. His solid weight, his light snore, the slight lime scent from his pillow. The old Tripp, the Tripp I'd miss.

But Tom and I both heard them coming in, Caroline and John, screaming at the girls huddled on the porch. Sydney apologizing, said *they'd just gone for a walk, that's all!* John's deep voice always pitched higher when he yelled, so unaccustomed to stretching that far.

"They simply went out to catch fireflies. I told them it was fine and to be back in an hour."

"You said it was *okay*?"

"Yes."

"I found them at the beach!" Caroline said.

"Well, there are fireflies at the beach," I replied.

"There was also a party at the beach," John said. "With much older kids."

"We weren't doing anything!" Sydney cried.

"Mom, we talked about this! There's a rapist out there. They are not allowed on the beach at night!"

"Caro," I started, then stopped. It would do no good to rile her up now. To remind her how she roamed as a child on Nantucket. Day and night. Without a cell phone, without a flashlight. Without a helmet on her bike. Dear God, the freedoms she'd had and taken for granted.

Tom's face was a mask of relief that he wasn't being blamed for once.

"There are fireflies in all the yards of this neighborhood," John said. "I don't see why you had to leave to catch them."

At that moment, I glanced at Courtney. Her jean shorts. A tank top under a hoodie. A bit of glitter around her eyes. She knew what she was doing, that Courtney. She was all hoverboard, that one. She gripped the pocket of her sweatshirt, tight, as if trying to lock it like a diary.

Tom and I exchanged a glance. He and I both knew: there was something in that pocket. A phone, a note, something.

From a boy who may or may not have been a rapist.

Well, we were leaving the next day. I'd send Tom and John to do a last check and lock up the other house. See if we'd left anything behind.

But what about what was left right in front of us?

Caroline

Later, I asked my daughter to help me take out the recycling to the car. It was just an excuse to get her away from Courtney, who I knew wouldn't volunteer to help. Courtney's hands had never touched garbage.

"Are you going to yell at me again?" Sydney asked.

"No," I said. "I just want to make sure that you're okay."

"I'm fine, Mom. I told you, nothing happened!"

"Honey," I said quietly, "a lot has happened."

And in that moment, away from her friend, away from the stern gazes of her grandmother, her face crumpled.

"Pop-pop," she said.

"Yes."

"It's so sad."

"It is. But he lived a long, happy life."

"But he never really got to know Courtney."

"Courtney?" I couldn't hide the surprise in my voice. Of all the things she could have said, could have thought.

I lifted her chin with my hand. Her eyes glistened with tears.

"Mom, he was so excited about her coming and about her hoverboard and all. It was his surprise, remember?"

"Yes."

"Do you think he would have liked her? After they spent more time together and stuff."

I sighed, swallowed. I tamped down everything that I could have said.

"Yes, honey," I said. "Of course."

"I guess we're not going to do the family portrait again, are we? Without Pop?"

I had completely forgotten. The day had come and gone. The end of an era.

"No, I guess not. It wouldn't be right, would it?"

"No. But we could do it, couldn't we? Just you and me and Dad? Maybe next year? Start our own tradition?"

"Yes, honey," I said. "We can start over."

Tom

The next morning, John and I went over to do a quick walk-through of the house before we left, like my mother had trained us all to do. God forbid we leave a nickel behind for the cleaning woman to find.

It was sunny, cloudless, windless. Finally getting warm, even at 7:00 a.m. The weather perfect, just in time for us to leave.

On the way, I told John what Matt had warned me about, whispering from his cell phone the day before, about the dented ladder. We all knew our ladder had that flaw, would match. Whoever accessed the roof from outside the house did it with our ladder.

"They'll get a search warrant," I said. "You know that. You know they will."

"Tom," John said, "you aren't suggesting…we get rid of it somehow?"

We stood on the corner of Charles and Hulbert. The house in front of us had one of those designs where you could see right through it, out to the water. Out to nothing. I'd always wanted a house like that, and now it seemed foolish, transparent. Nothing solid to hold on to.

"No," I sighed.

"She made you change that lightbulb," he said suddenly.

"What?"

"Remember? The day after we arrived? She insisted you do it, not me. She called you lazy—"

"John," I said. "Stop. She wouldn't—"

"And then," he said quietly, "she made you carry it back down to the basement."

"Dude, seriously."

He turned and walked toward the house, briskly, with purpose. He was taller than me, legs longer, and I had to struggle to keep up.

So we went down to the old house together. I didn't remember even changing the bulb, didn't remember my sister being any different that day compared to any other. They all blended together.

The blue front door was locked, which was shocking. We stood there, jiggling the doorknob as if we could change the outcome.

"Give me your key," John said.

"We shouldn't be here."

"It's your house, Tom. I think you can be here."

The house was cold and smelled a little moldy. It wasn't used to being closed, locked up tight. It needed air to circulate, to help all the old things feel new again. We walked through the kitchen, opened the creaky basement door. The stairway shook as we went down the stairs together, as if it were considering if it could hold the weight of us both.

In the corner, near the bikes, the silver ladder wobbled on its wall hook.

"It's just a coincidence, John," I said. "She always asks me to do shit like change lightbulbs. You know that."

"I hope you're right," he said. "But in case you're not."

He grabbed the ladder and pressed his hands and fingers on either side, firmly, cleanly, up and down, as if steadying someone's shoulders, saying *Hold on, buddy; we are all in this together.*

Then he steadied it, put it back where it was.

Matt

After one tenant leaves, before the next one arrives, I always stop by my houses. I schedule the cleaning crew in a wide enough window so that they have time to clean and I have time to make sure they've cleaned. And yes, sometimes that means I find the things they've missed. A crumb or two near the toaster. A milky ring underneath a vase. Dusting, wiping, sweeping—I've been known to do them all.

When I stopped by the cottage after the Warners had left for the ferry, I knew the cleaners hadn't been there yet. So I don't really know what I was looking for. The dishwasher had been run but not emptied. An oven mitt was askew on its hook. Upstairs, one toothbrush lay abandoned on the sink. I expected the bedroom to smell like Caroline still, that mix of shampoo and lotion or whatever it was that made her the way she was. But the windows had been left open a few inches, and the rooms smelled as damp and salty as anyone else's house. I closed them, lowered the shades to half-mast.

I went outside. The cottage next door was one of my houses too and was scheduled for rental August 1. Before that, there was bathroom tile to tear up and replace, fixtures that had to go, a laundry room to gut and renovate. I'd ordered a Dumpster a week ago, even though we wouldn't begin to fill it up, just because I didn't want to deal with the hassle of hauling small truckloads to the dump when it was busy season.

The workers weren't there yet, so I expected the Dumpster to be empty. I only looked inside because of it being after July 4. Habit, really. I needed to see if there were beer cans thrown in on the way to the beach, wine bottles, caps, something that belonged in recycling. But there weren't. It appeared to be empty.

But something made me look twice. There at the bottom, almost lining the metal, flattened cardboard from Cape Tile Works. From the first box of tile that had been delivered. I frowned; my guys knew better than to toss cardboard. But any pep talks about cleaning and recycling resulted in them calling me Mommy. Better to just clean up behind them and tease them later. But when I reached in to hook the corner of it, I stopped suddenly. Peeking beneath the damp cardboard, in the corner, part of a wooden handle.

I knew what that handle was. I didn't have to go in and retrieve it, didn't have to put my fingerprints on it. I saw the small telltale Sharpie dot on it, the system I'd devised. I'd assigned every client a color code for not only their keys, but every yard tool and dustbin and broom and rake—everything that might be used outside, everything that could accidentally end up in someone's truck. The only way to make sure things from the houses stayed in the houses.

Red was for the Warner house. Not this cottage, which was blue. Not the cottage next door, which was purple. I had a chart at home, a sample of all the colors, to keep track. Some clients had color combos, because I'd run out of colors as business picked up. My wife joked that it looked like something an art teacher would keep on a bulletin board, not a caretaker. She thought I enjoyed the color-coding a little too much. Still, if I didn't organize everything, keep track of it, things would get lost. It all could get lost.

So there it was. The axe from the Warners' basement. All anyone had to do was weaken the footings holding up that widow's walk. Notch those boards in a couple of places, and it would tumble down like a tree in a forest. Anyone with a logical brain could figure that out. You didn't have to be a contractor or an engineer.

I stood there between the two cottages, looking around. A tall hedge separated these properties from the lot behind them. A dirt road out front, more small cottages in every direction. No mansions, no estates on this side street, and that meant no alarms, no surveillance cameras. No one had seen me go into that Dumpster, but still I backed far off and stood watching it, as if it was on fire, throwing heat.

I left without the axe.

Would I have taken it, turned it in, under other circumstances? Maybe if I truly believed one of my crew had put it there. Or if I thought, as Alice did, that Bear Brownstein was going to jail. No. A man like Bear would have a lawyer smarter than Billy Clayton. And I knew as well as anyone that motive and opportunity didn't add up to guilt.

I walked to my truck and left. I parked down near the beach across from the Warners', walked down the public way, the grasses brushing at my legs, as if begging me to slow down. I sat down on the retaining wall and looked out at the harbor.

If I told my wife the whole story—which I can't and won't; I don't want to involve her in this any further with Billy Clayton threatening to interview her already—she would say not telling anyone about the Dumpster was self-preservation for us both, but she was wrong. It was my way of preserving Caroline as she was. Of going back in time and letting her be unblemished, unscarred. As perfect as she was at thirteen, always. Her husband would never know her that way. But I did. Once upon a time, I knew all her befores.

I watched as the fast ferry steamed through the harbor. If the widow's walk had still towered above the harbor, I could have gone up top, and Caroline could have seen me up there from the boat, waving. Waving like her parents always did, waving with red towels so she could see they were there.

I saw her—or imagined I did—three girls and a man, leaning against the railing on the outdoor deck, the salt spray deflected by her navy-blue windbreaker, looking back at her house. That had to be them. Hardly anyone else standing outside on this day when the weather chilled and threatened. Only an islander would do that.

But she didn't see me. It's possible, I know now, that she never really had. But I don't think of it that way. I like to think that it wasn't me that she walked away from but from that summer. From all of us who were there. And all of us who thought we knew.

Alice

These things do have a way of sorting themselves out. That's what I always told my children; maybe now they see that I am right. Everything is as it should be in the end. We'll repair the frayed and decaying house. The evil man who lives behind us will perhaps sell and go the Hamptons. Tripp is in a better place.

I was all alone at the house for a period of time on July 4. That wasn't orchestrated. It was inevitable. Anyone could have known that would happen. The innocent old lady. Had too much excitement and hubbub in town.

But I heard her that afternoon when we were all taking a nap. Up in the corridor, sleepwalking and dreaming like she'd done since she was a little girl. Her steps always light, like she was on tiptoe, ghosting her way through the house. I still remember the school counselor that year after the slumber party, trying to tell me that Caroline hadn't dreamed it, that she believed it was real. Four boys, not just one. But the evidence didn't support that. She'd had sex with someone but hadn't been injured. She hadn't screamed. But the child had been a dreamer since day one.

I saw the blades of grass stuck to the painted floor, dragged in on her dewy feet. *Sleepwalking outside*, I'd thought and made a note to mention it to John. Or maybe she simply went for a walk. I know better now. Out in the open, could have been doing a simple repair. It was all about picking your moment. There were other times I thought she was alone and could have gone back. When she'd run after Matt, for instance, and I was back in the kitchen, doing dishes.

All these years, I put my money on Tom, thinking he was the smartest, and I still believe he is, despite her brilliant treachery. Having a child, you see, has made her go strong and soft at the same time.

There is nothing like being a mother to make you do the things you didn't think you could do. It makes you choose one's word over the other on a summer night outside a tent. And it makes you eliminate anyone who threatens her, doesn't it, Caroline?

There's your motive, Billy Clayton, I think as I settle into the ferry and take out my crossword puzzles. Protecting my property was chickenfeed compared to Caroline protecting her child. Tripp was going down the tubes no matter what anyone did.

But Sydney was not going to go down with him. She was his chosen accomplice, and Caroline would have none of it.

And you know what? I don't blame her one bit. I'd have likely done the exact same thing in her spot. But will I tell on you, Caroline? Only if I have to. Not to save myself. Or Bear Brownstein.

But if I have to save Tom, I think we both know what I would do.

Tom

When the doctor came in and pronounced my father dead, the three of us were in the worst part of the hospital, the saddest room in the universe—the space where they deliver bad news. I remember it was painted a soothing shade of blue, which didn't matter. No one in that room ever sees anything. It's all about sound—what they hear, what they say, how they shriek.

We'd been sitting, and then we stood up to listen to the doctor, then to hug, shed tears. No point in sitting back down again. It didn't take long for the tears to stop, for pragmatism to creep in. In seconds, Caroline was blowing her nose, and Alice was out in the corridor, calling their island friends and Florida friends, sharing the news. John had stayed home with the girls. Caroline and I discussed next steps.

"I'll coordinate with Mom and make the arrangements," she said. "Maybe you could organize rearranging their condo, helping move his things. When she's ready."

"I'll call the golf club," I added. "And the one in Florida."

"Fine."

"Matt can help us with the house, of course."

"Yes, of course."

She got on her phone and tried to organize all our ferry reservations, and I let her.

I was sorry my father was dead. But I was glad to be leaving the island early; I couldn't lie about that. I was tired of watching him and being blamed when things went south. I was glad there was no family portrait and no family chowder dinner we did every July 5. The rest of the chowder would rot in the cottage refrigerator until Matt found it and emptied it. And I'm glad we didn't have to argue anymore about whether my dad was okay. Now, finally, we could agree.

And yes, I was glad I could finally take my phone off vibrate and answer the texts about the wine pairings for August parties and how they should outdo their friends. It's one big competition, wine collecting. Anyone who thinks it's about taste or terroir, or even about money, is fooling themselves. Competitiveness—that's how I made my money. It almost seemed destined. I understood that trait better than anyone. But being glad to return to work doesn't make me a monster. It makes me pragmatic, like dear old Mom.

"I've got to make a few work calls," I said. "Bring them up to speed, let them know I'll be out of pocket," I said, and she nodded.

Finally, we were both off the phone, and we decided to leave, called a cab.

We went out to the lobby. My clothes were damp, and I had streaks of blood up and down my sleeves from reaching down to check Dad's pulse. To lean in and tell him to hold on. He was still alive then, when I got to him, but barely. His head nodded slightly as if he heard me. *Hold on hold on hold on,* I'd said through my tears. Barely aware of anyone around me, my sister, John, the crowd that had begun to form. But had he held on up there, above the harbor? Or had he let go? *Squeeze my hand if you hear me, Dad,* I'd said. I thought I'd felt something, but maybe I was wrong.

Caroline's clothes looked cleaner than mine. Khakis were wrinkled, grimy at one knee, but no blood on her blue, cabled sweater. And her smell—that clean, strawberry smell she had... Well, I was grateful for it suddenly. It covered up whatever else had happened in the room.

We waited outside for the car to arrive. My mother was still on the phone, making her calls. There were other people outside on their phones too, other people waiting in their cars with the windows down. Several men paced up and down, adjacent to the sidewalk. Here were all the somber faces of Nantucket, right here, nowhere else. Even when the boat ride was choppy, even when the planes dipped in the wind, no one looked sad or worried. Unless they were here. Other people who'd received bad news or mixed news and were waiting for the next thing to happen, to figure out what to do or where to go. No one gave birth here. No one got life-saving cancer treatment here. This was for emergencies. This was the only truly sad place on Nantucket.

A cab driver pulled up. The driver got out and asked if we were the Reillys.

"Nope," I said, and he nodded. Some other poor family would be crying in his cab, not us.

He stretched elaborately while he waited, then looked inside at the lobby.

"They don't show up, I can take you," he said. "Where you headed?"

"Hulbert Avenue."

"Oh, you're a brave one."

"What do you mean?"

"All the rapists and vandals down thataway these days."

"Uh-huh."

"Hate crimes. Geez. That's a word nobody used ten years ago, right? A crime was just a crime."

Finally, the Reillys came out, carrying several plants and bouquets of flowers. They didn't look particularly sad, and I wondered if one of them had gotten an appendectomy or something. An emergency that required a stay, that beat the odds.

We watched them leave.

"We're lucky to get a ride home," I said. "Seeing as how Hulbert Avenue is now the ghetto."

"Right."

I asked Caroline something innocuous, stupid, changing the subject, if Sydney was ready for school. She shrugged, didn't answer, turned away. My mother stood at the other end of the sidewalk. She gestured with her right hand as she spoke, her gold bangles clinking. No Kleenex. No tears. All business.

"Let me ask you something else," I said. "Are you going to be mad at me forever?"

"Shut up," she said.

"No. I think I have a right to know how long this shit is going to go on. Through adulthood, and childbirth, and now death?"

"Why are you rehashing this?"

"Because you rehash it every day we are together. Every day."

"I do not."

"You do."

"Do you have any idea," she said suddenly, "what it's like to grow up with no one in your family believing you?"

"I believe you."

"Yeah, right. That's why you told the police Connor Grinstaff was at a party that night. That you saw him walking there."

"I thought I did."

"Well, you thought wrong."

"And I have apologized to you for that."

"And who cares who it was, Tom? If it was him or just others? It happened, and you didn't stop it!"

"I don't know what you're—"

"How could you not have heard? *How?*"

"Caroline! You said he *covered your mouth*, that his hands smelled dirty, that—"

"The walls in that house are made of paper! Mom could hear me when I coughed!"

Caroline was the only person I knew who could look exactly like she was crying yet shed no tears. Her face, as pained as I'd ever seen a face, as sad and full of mourning as you could imagine, was dry.

I took a deep breath. "Do you have any idea how close a giggle and a cry are?"

"What?"

"The sound," I said. "The difference between a girl crying and giggling, to a guy, the line is paper thin. I don't think you realize how close they are. Not just when you're young, but now. Still. I get up in the middle of the night sometimes, when we're all together here, and listen outside Sydney's room, just to try to make sure I've heard it right. Just to be sure she's okay."

"You do?"

"See? You don't believe me either."

"Touché," she said softly. Or at least that's what it sounded like. Because suddenly, finally, my sister seemed tired, spent, soft.

"And I know, Caroline, why you didn't fight back as hard as people thought you would. Because I know the difference between guys who are there because they like you and guys who are there because they are taking advantage of you is hard to measure."

"Spoken like someone who has taken advantage of a few girls."

"Look, I know how young you were. I saw girls in college, twenty years old, who couldn't figure it out either. And I know that Matt wasn't the only boy you liked that summer. I know you were just…practicing."

She took a deep breath. "Do me a favor, Tom."

"Sure."

"Don't you ever, ever fucking say that to him."

Maggie Sue

An island is a terrible place to commit a crime. You can't get on or off without buying a ticket. Us locals notice every last little thing, every blade of grass out of place. What else is there to do? There's nowhere to hide your secrets, except the water, and then, well, the tide always comes in. You can count on that.

I imagine the footage from all the fancy video cameras on Hulbert Avenue—and there were dozens—showed plenty. More than enough. Too much. People tromping across other people's lawns. People cutting through, people going places. Neighbors and friends. Fathers and daughters. Shadows and light.

But what would that prove? Nothing, that's what. Not a blessed thing. Except that here, everyone had sand between their toes, dune grass on the bottoms of their feet, hair tousled from the wind, memories hazy from the fog. And secrets, we all had them.

People carried matches in their pockets, flasks. People had cases of wine in their cars. People took extra trips to the dump, wore gloves because it was cold at night.

What could you do? What could you prove?

Like it sometimes does, it comes down to who you want to believe, who you want to protect, and who you want to hurt. When it all comes out even, and everyone gets what they wanted, who do you blame? They all lied, cheated, screwed up, covered up. Even the kid.

The way I figure it, Alice Warner mowed her own swastika, and no matter what Caroline said or where she was or where they knew Tripp Warner might have been heading, the widow's walk was old and out of code and could have fallen down at any time. They're just lucky it was the old man and not the kid, or all of them, crowded up there to watch the fireworks. The smartest thing that family did was watch that display from the beach, down below.

And it doesn't have anything to do with anything, but Billy Clayton, I'll admit it now. *I did like him*, you were right.

Sometimes I went into his closet just to look at his clothes.

He never left anything on the floor or on a chair; it was either in the laundry room or hung up, folded. He had nice things, and he appreciated them, and I admired that. I'd seen a few too many homes with cashmere sweaters crumpled into balls, with suede shoes kicked off, down jackets that cost more than a sleeping bag thrown like they were nothing. They weren't nothing, and he knew that.

So yes, I stood among the wools, the fine cottons, the camel's hair, the silk ties. Things hung by color, type, like a store. I spaced out the wooden hangers sometimes so they were even, placed my fingers between them like a comb, going up and down the line. I dusted the tops of his shoe trees, the knobs that held his belts and ties. But mostly I just breathed in, the male and clean and decent scent of him, leather and wool and shaving cream. No cologne, no extras, just enough. I breathed in that closet and wondered why there weren't more like it, used as the designers intended, neat and tidy, like a photo. I wanted to take a photo sometimes, but I didn't. That would be too creepy.

My work *was* creepy sometimes, it was. Sometimes I felt like a burglar or worse, looking under their beds, inside their drawers. You go through the motions, don't think twice about it, until, suddenly, you do. You think about the knowledge you have, the intimacy, the power. I could put tacks on their desk chair, acid in their shampoo. I could poison their food.

And sometimes I wanted to.

There was a guest at the Grinstaffs' Daffodil weekend who left yellow nail polish all over the sink. I mean, really, who polishes their nails over the sink? I didn't even know how to remove it; I had to call my friend Molly who does nail art at the salon on Center Street and ask her what in the bejesus to do. It just had to be done, fixed. No extra time, no extra money. And no murdering of the person who did it.

One time I was at the Brownsteins', I was in his closet when I heard the door, thank God. I grabbed my bucket of supplies and went downstairs.

"Are you okay?" Bear asked.

"Yes, why?"

"You look a little flushed."

"Oh, the hot water and all," I said.

"Do you need to sit down, take a break?"

"Nah."

"Would I be in your way if I went upstairs while you finish down here?"

"Of course not," I said breezily. "It's your house."

"But you're in charge," he said and smiled.

As he walked past me, I felt my cheeks redden further. No one ever asked if they would be in my way. No one else ever said I was in charge.

No one else ever asked how I *was*.

Tom

I was walking up the beach from Brant Point in 1987, dragging a kayak, when I saw my father step onto Connor Grinstaff's back porch. Their enormous house, right on the water with a view of the lighthouse, took up two lots. The furniture on that porch, I know now, was worth more than anything inside our house. But as a boy, all of it was just a big gray something I passed on the way to the boat, to the beach, to a party at the lighthouse.

My eyesight was 20/20 then, so if I wanted to see something, I could. I knew my dad's gait, his gestures, his shock of light-brown hair, lifted by cowlicks, standing taller than other people's fathers. And I recognized his bright-yellow golf shirt. Unmistakable. Ugly. Almost neon. I was less remarkable, a blond boy in bleached Nantucket red bathing trunks, one of many, a dime a dozen. I'd proven myself to be just that unremarkable, time after time. Especially that summer. Not a golden boy, just a boy. Just another idiot.

Something made me creep closer, then stop, sit, watch from behind a dinghy overturned on the beach. As if I knew that walking by might change something important.

This was where he lived. Connor, a few years older than me, the one I said I'd seen walking toward the party down at the lighthouse, not toward our house in the opposite direction. He had dark hair that was long on top and short everywhere else, like a preppy surfer, and a way of flipping it back with one hand that seemed both cool and, in hindsight, ridiculous, a tic. It was that motion, that flick, that I thought I'd seen under the streetlight on July 5. But it turns out he was just as unremarkable as I was. He could have been anywhere, anyone.

His sister was Caroline's friend. Pippa, her name was. She was at the slumber party. They don't call them that anymore— *sleepovers*, I know, is the current term. Doesn't matter, really, because neither of them is accurate. They should be called wakeovers, because the point was not to sleep, not at all. The other boys who'd come with Connor that night, the pack of three, or five—no one knew the number—probably lived nearby too. I didn't know their names, but I'd seen them in their Jeep and their boat, hanging out at the yacht club, spreading out and taking over at Children's Beach with their beers and their joints when night fell, like a gang claiming territory.

The tide was coming in; the wind was coming up. It sang loudly in my ears, like the inside of a shell. I couldn't hear words, cars, the slam of a screen door. I saw Dad's yellow shirt appear, like a bobbing bright kite. Connor and his father were waiting for him. Then Dad motioned to someone in the driveway behind him, lingering on the porch stairs, and then, slow as a ghost, my sister appeared. She was thirteen but looked older. She'd always looked older, because there was a seriousness about her, even then.

She mostly kept her head down the whole time. She didn't wipe away any tears, but she didn't look them in the eye, didn't gesture, didn't scream. She didn't leave, though. She didn't refuse to come. Why? She stood there throughout what must have been an apology. A negotiated agreement. No pressing charges. No nasty investigation. Connor, who must have been going into his senior year at prep school, would go to his Ivy League college the next year, would graduate. But would he change? Every so often over the years, I'd Google the family's name, to see if he'd ever been arrested. If he'd done something the same, similar, or worse. But there was nothing. He disappeared.

It was only a few minutes. They didn't sit down. Finally, my sister nodded and looked up. And in her face, I saw it. The blush. The embarrassment. She liked this boy, and it was just too much to bear. She turned to go. And then, in the few seconds my father trailed behind, he turned slightly and gripped Connor by the shoulder. How hard did he squeeze? Was it like one of those handshakes that let you know who was boss? I don't know. I hope so, but somehow I doubt it. All I know is that whatever my father's last words to him were—*I hope you learn a lesson from this, Son* or *It took courage to apologize*—that he punctuated it with a wink. A classic Tripp Warner wink.

And my sister, turning back to see if my father was coming, must have seen it too.

I stood there now, knocking on the door of that same damned house. The clouds were coming in offshore, and it was cold, too cold for a beach day. It was also early, too early for a teenager to be anywhere but home. I just had to see for myself. I'd stolen Courtney's phone off the porch when they were sleeping, so I already knew the boy they'd met on the beach had been the musician from July 4. His name was Jeremy, and he was easy to find—all over Instagram and Snapchat promoting his music. Long hair, skinny. That's not who I was looking for. I was looking for a kid named Carter, whose Facebook settings were set to public, a kid whose photos led you to believe he idolized his father, even if he'd lost the family house in a bitter divorce.

When Maggie answered the door, I wasn't surprised exactly. And she didn't seem surprised either when I asked for the boy, not the mother, not the father. We both knew the door had been open, and I could have walked in and found him myself.

"Carter? He's downstairs playing video games. The sound is so damned loud, I can almost hear 'em over the vacuum."

I nodded. Lazy. Violent. Probably hadn't read a book since kindergarten. Nantucket's finest.

"Can you tell him to come out here for a minute?"

"I can try."

She went to the basement door and called down several times, saying someone wanted to talk to him outside. He loped to the door in that unsteady way adolescent boys do, boys who grew too fast one summer. He wasn't fit, athletic like his father. Not yet anyway.

"You Carter Grinstaff?"

"Yeah."

"How old are you?"

"Who are you?"

"I'm your neighbor. How old are you now?"

"Fifteen."

"Rising sophomore?"

"Freshman."

I nodded. Typical. Hold 'em back so they could crush at sports. But this kid looked like he was headed for the chess club.

"How tall are you?"

"What? Who are you again?"

"Just verifying your age and your...attributes," I said and smiled.

"No. Wait, are you like a census taker or something?"

"Something like that."

"I'm five foot three and a half."

"Thanks, you can go back to your intellectual pursuits. Unless your dad is down there with you? Because I'd like to beat the shit out of him if you don't mind."

"What? Cleaning woman!" he yelled. "This man here is threatening me!"

"Calm down," Maggie said as she came back in.

"Her name is Maggie," I said. "You got that? Now get the fuck out of here."

He left, fingering his phone, and I hoped I hadn't just gotten her in trouble.

"He's a charmer, isn't he? Typical only child. No offense to your niece."

"None taken. He been here all summer?"

"Yup."

"Has he gotten a haircut recently? Or dyed it, like the kids do?"

"Nope. Short, dark hair just like his old man. Why you asking, if you don't mind me knowing."

"Just making sure he isn't a tall, floppy blond-haired asshole assaulting girls on the beach."

"Well, he's an a-hole all right. But he's a short, dark-haired a-hole."

Everyone else left that day but me. I drove their stuff to the ferry, but they insisted on walking. Left the Jeep in the driveway as they always did, leaving Matt to store it for the winter. Funny to think about the season ending for my mother so early. What would she do with herself? Would she travel, go somewhere cooler with friends? I shook John's hand, hugged my mother and Sydney good-bye, and stood across from my sister, took a deep breath. I knew better than to hug her; we'd stopped doing that long ago.

"It's not him," I said simply.

"Who?" she said with alarm in her voice.

"The rapist at Steps. It's not Grinstaff's kid."

"Wait—what?"

"In case you thought history could repeat itself. He doesn't match the description, at all. Not one bit."

"How do you know?"

"Billy Clayton deputized me."

"Yeah, right."

I shrugged. "You think all I do is drink wine and guard old men? I'm a bundle of surprises, Caroline."

"Should I start calling you Peeping Tom?"

"Very funny. I just went over there, and Maggie let me have a look at him."

"Jesus, does she clean every house on Brant Point?"

"Possibly. She probably makes more money than either of us. Anyway, this kid is dark-haired and shorter than Sydney."

"Maybe he has a brother."

"He doesn't."

"Well, whoever did it, I hope Billy Clayton catches the fucker before we come back next summer."

"Or before he does," I said and smiled.

"It's not funny, Tom."

"I know."

She said she'd be in touch about Dad's funeral. Logistics. The service. Who would speak first and what topics she'd want me to cover. I pitied, for a moment, the director of the church. The details, the control, the haranguing.

"Sounds good," I said. "Safe travels."

They left me there alone. The car ferry wasn't till later, and the house and cottage were already locked up tight. I had nothing but time. I started up the Audi and drove in the opposite direction of the harbor. I drove past all the tourists on Main Street, past all the trucks out at Marine Home Center, past the cyclists at the Rotary. I drove out to Polpis Road and over to Altar Rock.

I thought I would drink a toast to the old man, for better or worse, for his trying to do the right thing but failing, always, like we all did in Alice's or Caroline's eyes. For traveling where we hadn't, doing the reconnaissance for us, doing the right thing and the wrong thing all at once. For jumping up and down to make sure it could hold our weight. And it couldn't.

But at the last minute, I didn't feel like drinking.

The drive was shorter than I'd remembered. It had been years since I'd been there with a car, and it had been at night probably. Drunk. There were no other cars on the dirt road. I got out of the car and left the bottle and the corkscrew in the trunk. I walked up the gravel path to what had always felt like the dead center of the island, the highest point, and turned in circles, taking in a view in every direction, just like our widow's walk.

Ocean and dunes and lighthouses in two directions. Moors and cranberry bogs in between. I reached in my pocket for my phone and took a quick video of the panorama. Sydney would want to see this. She was old enough now to see the full attributes of this spot. The remoteness, the specialness. She was old enough to ride her bike out here alone, party with kids, misbehave. But I wouldn't show her. The video, I knew, was just for me.

The clouds were coming in from the west; they would not be ignored. Rolling in, moving on my watch, dotting blue sky with gray, casting shadows across the curving dark-green moors, the pale dune grasses. Everything about to be more vibrant just before it fell into shadow. The changing light on this island could take your breath away. Is that what did it, I wondered? My father's breaths, literally taken from him by beauty?

My father loved Altar Rock because other people overlooked it, drove right past. Let the tourists stay on the edges, burrow in the sand. We are up and away from the others, so we can see, so we could know. Maybe so we can learn. And find a way home to how we all used to be. My father and mother, in love once. My sister and I getting along just fine. The neighbors taking care of one another in their own way. Pooling their resources, their gin and their clams and their boats and their bicycles. Not fighting over the ocean, over what everyone knew wasn't theirs.

I don't know precisely what my father was looking for as he started his climb that spring and summer. All those stairs, over and over. Maybe he simply knew what was happening, what was coming. That he wasn't well. That there was something else wrong with him and his wife was going to have to lock him up, or in, or down. That his granddaughter was not going to follow him wherever he went, that he would not be granted a second chance.

So he just kept trying, kept seeking higher ground. Until it gave way. Or maybe, just maybe, until he found the courage to fly.

I could learn a few lessons, still, from the old man. It was time for me to vacation somewhere else, away from my family, where my clients couldn't find me and people didn't look at me and see a child. It was time for me to sleep on a bed I paid for myself and follow my own itinerary. And I would do that, soon. But probably not in July.

Caroline

I t was cold on the ferry; the clouds had started to roll in, threatening. Too soon to say if it was going to rain or pass over. If our ride back to Hyannis would be bouncy or smooth. The weather forecast, the predictions, the calculations for Nantucket and the islands were always just a little bit off when you listened in advance. Better to look at your own barometer, to stand in the wind, to wait.

"Put on your jackets, girls," I said as we headed to the outdoor deck. And what a relief that was, given what Courtney was wearing. A tank top that dipped a little too low and showed the edge of a bright-blue bra. A colored bra, not beige or white or even black. Surely a blue bra was one of the first signs of the apocalypse.

Sydney, Courtney, and John and I each had a penny in our right hand to throw at the bell buoy. My mother stayed inside, but I had an extra penny for her in my left hand. This was our Nantucket tradition, to ensure that you come back to the island. You threw your penny at the last bell buoy as you departed on the ferry. Other natives threw it earlier, at Brant Point. If you knew about this island secret. If you were a local, that is.

Courtney struggled not to roll her eyes as we explained it to her.

"So it's like a wishing well," Courtney said. "Or a fountain for, like, babies at the mall."

"No," John said. "It's an ancient mariner's tradition. And the pennies buried below turn a rainbow of green and blue from the algae, develop barnacles over time, like sunken treasure. Scuba divers would give anything to go down and see them, but the area is protected by the Cousteau Foundation."

"Yeah," Sydney said.

"That is complete and utter bullshit," I whispered to him, smiling.

"Sometimes you have to fight adolescence with bullshit," he replied.

John leaned down and gave the girls advice on timing, aim, trajectory. They stood in the wind, eyes fixed on the furthest buoy. The boat pitched up and down in the wind, and we all caught a little spray. The girls squealed, and John cried, "Now! Throw them now!"

One by one, we cocked our arms and let go. The wind made it impossible to get close; the pennies were light, faltered, and fell too close to the boat. No matter. Tradition was tradition. I transferred my mother's penny to my right hand and threw it last.

"Seems so strange not to throw one for your dad," John said.

"Yes."

"Maybe we could bury him with a penny? As a final gesture."

I swallowed hard to try to keep from crying. "That is a lovely idea," I said finally, quietly.

"You know, when I packed up your dad's clothes to go to the cottage," John said, "I found pennies and wire cutters in his drawer. Isn't that strange?"

"Wire cutters? Maybe the renters left them."

"No, I knew they were his, because of the red dot."

"What?"

"All the tools in the house are color coded with a little red dot."

"They are not."

"They are. It's Matt's system. To keep the houses straight. He does it so small, the owners don't notice."

"He told you that?"

"Alice did. The first year I came to the island. I think she enjoyed going on and on about Matt. Keeping me on my toes," he said and smiled.

"We have to go back," I said, my voice rising, urgent, breaking.

"What?"

"We have to go back!"

"Well, of course we will, honey. Every year. To honor your Dad, to—"

"No, I mean when we get to Hyannis. We have to turn around and go straight back on the next boat."

And he didn't ask why, and he didn't ask if I forgot something. He nodded, as if he knew. As if he was already prepared to cover for me, to make this right, and knew what to say to the girls if we had to stay another night or two.

And then he hugged me tight anyway.

Alice

Alone in Hyannis, I walked a few blocks to my car. Caroline said she'd forgotten her phone and charger, and they all lined up to go back on the fast ferry without me, at my insistence. God forbid a person live a day without their phone!

I'd been on the boat long enough. I'd been on the island long enough. I was ready to go home. Oh, the original plan was for us to caravan as we travelled south; John would drive my car, Caroline would go with the girls. They could settle me on the car train to Florida and feel they'd done their duty looking after the grieving widow.

"I'm fine," I assured John.

"I am totally fine circling back alone," Caroline said. "You all could wait here, at the mini golf."

"I'm not waiting," I said. "You go."

John glanced at her, at me, at the girls in his care.

"John, I drove here, remember? All the way."

"Yes, but you weren't…"

He stopped short of saying *alone*. Well, we would all have to get used to saying it now, wouldn't we? I was alone, right and truly.

I grasped his hand. "I promise to stop in Connecticut."

But oh, the look on his face as they left nearly crushed me. The steamship ticket window tucked under a gazebo, the people lining up to pay. Following his wife and the girls, then glancing back at me as I watched. The tenderness and worry on his face. His hand raised gallantly to wave one last good-bye. I saluted, trying to lighten the moment.

Oh, I'd tried so hard not to weep, not to spray the children's grief with a drop of my own! And then, his kindness. His innocence.

The tears started down my cheeks as I rolled my suitcase up to the lot and located my car. We parked at the same place every year, an old dilapidated house with a double lot that fit cars in every nook and cranny. What would it be like, to live there with all those vehicles everywhere? The constant comings and goings, the revvings and backings up? I realized, suddenly, that Tripp would love it. The energy, all the people to talk to, the goings on.

We were opposites, and now my opposite was gone. And what is a person without that oppositional pull? Would I be less myself or more, without that magnetism by my side?

I turned on the car, adjusted the air-conditioning, and sat in the driver's seat with the windows up, alone. I let the tears fall. I wept in the anonymity of that vehicle as the strangers walked by with their golf clubs and tote bags, as the cars came and went.

Then I blew my nose and headed for the highway, for the Braziers' house. Three and a half hours, tops. I had quite a story to tell; not all of it of course, just part. No one knows the whole story, just pieces. Not even me.

That day at Surfside, Tom and Caroline asked me what else had happened that I hadn't told them about. What had made me so afraid. Until Tripp grabbed the keys to that surf van and drove away, they hadn't seen what I'd seen.

No. They hadn't been with us that night in West Palm at the community center, having after-dinner drinks with the other couples on "our cellblock" as Tripp liked to call it. If you could call a three-bedroom condominium with indoor/outdoor pools, a swim-up bar, and a kitted-out health club a prison. The weather was unbearably hot already in June. Many of our friends had left by Memorial Day, gone to Maine or New Jersey or Michigan or wherever they planned to summer. We didn't like to arrive on Nantucket too early, because it was cold. We weren't getting older; we were merely getting pickier, not settling for anything until it was the perfect temperature.

Six of us for dinner, then brandy. The men went out for a cigar, and of course, Tripp wasn't allowed to smoke anymore. That set him off, I thought, but that was before I knew anything. That was when I still believed, fully, in logic.

He disappeared. That's what the men said when they came back in from the balcony, smelling of smoke and liquor. The three women, Lizbeth and Fran and I, looked at each other as if we could find him between us, in the air.

"Did he go to the restroom?"

"We already looked there."

"He must have gone back to the condo," I said, because what else could be concluded?

We called his cell phone, but of course, he didn't answer. No one our age answered our phones; they were in our pockets to call out, not pick up.

I was on my way back to our condo, walking down the glass-walled corridor—like a fishbowl really, the design of the place, so everyone could see what was going on all of the time, even when it was nobody's damned business—when the activity director, Karen, came up beside me, speaking in hushed tones. Told me that my husband was creating a disturbance, and the police had been called.

A disturbance. Oh, we were used to downplaying things in my family, in my world; God knows I'd painted over every minor and major infraction over the years with an insouciance that bordered on playacting. But Karen's phrase really took it to a new level.

Tripp was standing on the roof, eight stories up, peeling off his clothes, screaming that it was too damned hot and to go away, damn it! Laughing, as if it was the best party trick of all time.

The police had been kind, gentle. Used to this sort of thing in this state of retirees and crazies, I suppose. But the retirement community association had put us on notice. A formal evaluation was required. There could be no more incidents. Tripp would not be allowed to reside there, depending on the findings. Depending on the future.

So what did I do? I did the only thing I could think of. I stayed on our schedule and drove north. In my own defense, I thought it was an aberration. I thought it was the alcohol and the heat and the cigar smoke. Even I would not have attempted driving with him along if I'd known it was only going to get worse. There were moments when he was docile and fine. And in the end, didn't he deserve one last time on the island, no matter what impediments there were? He had been there every summer of his life. He knew nothing else, ever. To keep him away seemed criminal, cruel.

So yes, I put it all off. All the evaluating, the tests, whatever. I drove him to an island with limited services and thought we could handle it within the family. Procrastination in favor of routine.

I'd thought I'd warned the children sufficiently without creating undue panic. I thought if we banded together and shared our perspectives that collectively, we'd figure out exactly what to do.

And yes, I'll admit it. In the end, it came down to this: salt water. Sea air.

We'd always believed that was the cure for anything.

And who is to say that we weren't right?

Matt

My crew was still a little hungover from the holiday weekend. I could tell by the way they walked, like they were dragging their feet through silt, spartina. Not enough coffee in the world to make things right. That's the thing about starting work early; there's nowhere to hide. Tired is normal, but usually after a few cups of coffee, everyone was functioning. But not that day. They were struggling, and me, always trying to be one of the guys, I pitched in to help with the cottage renovations.

They tore up the old tile and fixtures from the master bathroom while I helped Jimmy lay the new tile in the first-floor powder room. That was the most important, after all, because that's what their guests would use. Let the still-drunks do the demo; they couldn't screw that up too badly. But laying tile was a sober man's job.

So we worked in tandem, Jimmy and I, in a rhythm, making up for lost time, cutting the glass tiles to fit in the corners, around the toilet, the pedestal sink. Everyone wanted glass tile and a pedestal sink in a small powder room; it's as if it was written on some coastal manual somewhere.

When I finished, I watched with satisfaction as the other guys ferried the old crap out to the Dumpster and threw it over the side with a satisfying clunk and crash. The toilet and tub cracking. All of it hiding what was below. Three-quarters of the way filled, but that was enough for me. I called the Dumpster company and told them it was full, and if they could pick it up and take it out to the dump before tomorrow, that would be great.

I had just hung up and was walking to my car when Billy Clayton pulled up. No lights flashing, no hurry.

"Hey, Matt," he said.

"Hey, Billy."

I took a breath, exhaled. Didn't want to breathe too deeply. Didn't want to give anything away. Tried to stay as nonchalant as possible, despite my belief that this guy was a fucking clairvoyant or something. We were thirty feet from the Dumpster.

"Question for you," he said.

"Yeah?"

"The Warners out of the cottage you let them borrow?"

"Yeah."

It was a ridiculous question. I was sure he knew exactly where they were, when they left. I imagined him trying to stop them from leaving town, imagined Alice telling him the only way to stop her was to arrest her. But surely he knew what boat they were on. One word to the Steamship Authority could have taken care of that.

"Mind if I take a look around?"

His eyes were on the cottage next door. Not the one we were working on. Not the Dumpster out back. Was he trying to fool me with this?

"I don't mind," I said.

"Great," he said and started for the front door. Walking slowly across the grass, like he wasn't worried. Like I wasn't gonna stop him.

"But my clients," I called after him. "The owners of that cottage? They'd mind. Without a warrant in your hand, they'd mind quite a bit."

He stopped, turned. I swear there was a smile on his face.

A call came in on his phone, and I watched him answer, heard his response. Another attack on the beach, but a suspect in custody.

"Well, looks like you got some bigger fish to fry," I said.

"Yeah," he said. "Lots of fish this week."

He put on his flashing lights, turned them on as casually as another person might turn on a porch light, and was long gone when they came to pick up the Dumpster.

And so was I. I left Jimmy there to wait for the Dumpster guy, so he was the one who called me and said as they were loading it up, Caroline came running up the lane and watched as they took it away. He asked if she was okay, and she said she'd forgotten something in the house.

"I told her I didn't have the key to that one. But that you'd go through it and mail anything you found back to her. Is that okay?" Jimmy asked.

"Yes," I replied. "If I find anything of hers, I'll send it."

**FROM THE DESK OF LIEUTENANT
BILLY CLAYTON**

Notes on Arrest of Jeremy Mattson, July 6, 2017,
  4:00 p.m.
Suspect apprehended at Jetties Beach parking lot
  after victim provided a detailed description
Said she'd seen him twice before, once at a beach
  party, and once playing guitar on Main Street
ID'd in lineup
Suspect demanded a lawyer. Placed call to father's
  firm in Philadelphia

Tom

O ne more thing I had to do before I left. Something I should
have done myself instead of leaving it in my mother's hands
or Matt's.

I was the man of the house now, for better or worse.

I left my car around the corner. His Range Rover wasn't in
the driveway, but another car was: a white Lexus. I walked up the
smooth, clean stairs, knocked on the glass door.

I asked the woman who answered if Bear was home, and she
said he was golfing and would be back at dinnertime. She wore
no makeup or shoes, and her sleeves were rolled up. Probably his
personal chef or florist.

"If you'd like to come back then perhaps?" she said politely.

"I'm leaving on the four o'clock boat," I said. "If you'd just
tell him that... Um..." My own name caught with shame in my
throat. "That Tom Warner stopped by."

"Oh my goodness," she said, her hand going up to her heart.
"I'm so sorry about your father, about all of it, really."

"If you'd tell him I just wanted to introduce myself. Extend...
an olive branch. Or an olive in a martini. Something."

"Well, I'll tell him we met. I'm Binky."

"Binky?"

"His wife."

"Binky Brownstein?" I said, suddenly worried I had the wrong house. This woman was blond and wearing a sweater with patched elbows.

"Oh, I go by my maiden name. Binky Vanderbilt."

I swallowed hard, coughed uncontrollably. She offered me a tissue, a glass of water. But that wouldn't help. What helps when you are trying your damnedest not to burst out laughing?

Matt

I didn't see her the night it happened in 1987. She couldn't call. And everyone had their hands full, driving all the girls home, taking Caroline to the hospital, talking to the police. And arguing. Arguing over who did what, who had been where. And of course, they wouldn't think to call me, of all people. We'd tried our damnedest to hide from them. I wasn't sure they even knew my name back then, this townie friend of her brother's. But I should have known that I couldn't keep anything from Alice and Tripp Warner. She told me everything, afterward.

No. It couldn't have been Connor. Tom saw him walking to the party.

From his window, yes. Under the streetlight.

Could you be mistaken?

Well, perhaps you were dreaming.

You've always been a sleepwalker, darling.

We would have heard something, surely.

She has a boyfriend, yes. Matt Whitaker.

I don't know if they've been sexually active or not, but it's a distinct possibility.

Yes, that would explain it. Of course it would.

But we hadn't. I'd thought about it, thought about it night and day, as boys do, but she wasn't ready. We'd done just about everything else, but she was younger than I was, and I was willing to wait. I would have waited a lifetime for her. But they didn't know that, and they used it against her.

And me? Well, I made a mistake too. Instead of telling her I would take my father's hunting rifle and shoot them all—which is what I considered later that day and every day for weeks—I did the stupidest thing ever. I said the most wrong, dunderheaded, selfish thing I could have said. Her family, me, the police, we all screwed up, and she never forgave us. It ended that day for her, but never for me.

I wanted to be your first, I said, tears stinging my eyes.

Everything I've done since, for her, for her family, was to erase those words. I buff them out, year after year, and still, like a tattoo, they remain.

So I fixed their house in August, the roof, the gaping holes, the ripped gutters, the bent porch railing. The neighboring houses were full of children and houseguests; the Brownsteins had their daughter's wedding on their lawn and rented a whole row of houses for their family. God only knows how much that cost, renting four houses in August. But I didn't care. I didn't even see them around me.

I sawed and nail-gunned and hammered away from dusk to dawn, not caring if I was waking up everyone at 7:00 a.m. I hired out the rest of my caretaking work to other guys, delegated all the stupid calls to replace an outdoor umbrella that had blown away or to drain a pool after a kid shit in it. No, the Warners needed me. The house needed me.

I didn't want their roof to start leaking before the widow's walk could be sorted out, to ruin the third floor, everyone's favorite, with the best light and the faraway views. Couldn't have that. As terrible as it was, Tripp's fall gave me a chance to upgrade their gutters and redo the pitch of the porch railing. Things they'd never bother to pay for, things I'd always wanted to do, I did. In many ways, the house had never looked better.

I went to the board meeting with the Warners' lawyer from the

Cape, and he asked for the widow's walk to be rebuilt at the same height, to be grandfathered in. It was built before they changed the height restriction—or so we said. We didn't really know, and Old Bobby couldn't remember. As if a ghost had built it, as if it had simply risen one day through the roof. It was taken under advisement. We'll see what they say and try to rebuild in the autumn. And everything will be like new come next July.

And when the lawyer said those words, a chill went down my spine. *Grandfathered*. God help me, what a phrase that is to me now. I couldn't bear to tell Alice on the phone, couldn't say it. She said the autopsy had indicated Tripp had had a brain tumor. The cancer spread. Making him behave like someone we did and didn't know. Probably had been there for year, hiding, and no one knew. The signs were all there, she said, as if I didn't know that. As if she was finally admitting it to herself.

Grandfathered. I don't think I'll ever say that word again. Or widow's walk.

We all need to watch what we say, and what we mean, and how we behave. And be careful, very careful, what we wish for when we reach for the heights. Whether it's a girl who's out of your league, or a job, or a deck built on top of a house just a little too high.

Because it can be a long, very long way down. And an even longer climb back up.

The tradition of taking a Warner family photo has ended for good, I suppose. But I can imagine what the next one would look like, the burdens lifted for some. Alice looking lighter, maybe Caroline and Tom too. Who knows?

But portrait or not, they'll be here next July. So will their house. Alice will come first, stay the summer. The others will come for as long as they can stand to be around each other. I bought them a new ladder and a new axe for their firewood. The wood on them is still blond, fresh.

And me? Well, I'm not going anywhere.

I smile as I say this. Because wasn't that precisely the problem?

FROM THE DESK OF GEORGE EVERHART

July 10, 1987

Interview notes, Caroline Warner investigation, Billy Clayton, Buck Clayton's son

Name came up as matching description of possible assailant

Boy claims he was down at the White Elephant washing dishes 5:00 p.m.–11:00 p.m. on July 4

Time clock, supervisor at restaurant supports

Saw group of boys walking up Willard toward him, laughing

Could have come from Hulbert

Said it was dark but he "recognized one of the boy's laughs" from beach party at Grinstaffs' the weekend before

Said he was certain. Said Connor Grinstaff's laugh was "distinctive"

Admits it was dark. Almanac confirms quarter moon that night, clouds

No positive ID

Reading Group Guide

1. The anniversary of trauma is a central theme in *The Fifth of July*. Have you ever experienced this kind of pain or stress as the anniversary of a death or violent event approaches?

2. The divisions between summer people and year-rounders are starkly evident in this story. Are there other places in the country or world where you have noticed these differences?

3. The metaphor of fixing people's houses versus fixing people's lives pervades the novel. Have you ever noticed parallels in your community between what people do to their houses and what they do to themselves?

4. Several of the characters in the book remain fixated on, or stymied by, events and relationships from when they were teenagers. Why is it so hard to move past the memories of these tender years?

5. Though set on the relatively crime-free island of Nantucket, the novel showcases a wide variety of minor and major crimes, from vandalism to theft to rape and murder. Is this realistic? And do beautiful places do a better job of hiding ugly behavior?

6. The book highlights sharp disagreements with religious overtones, bordering on criminality, yet none of the characters seems particularly religious. What does this say about the growth and inheritance of prejudice?

7. The Warners are a family uncomfortable with talking about things, whether good or bad. What events in the book could have been aided or avoided by an open discussion?

8. The island lifestyle of unlocked doors, moonlit beach walks, and talking to friendly strangers brings up different issues of trust and vulnerability for different ages. Have you ever felt threatened in an environment like this? If so, why?

9. Tripp Warner's illness is perceived and handled differently by each character in the book. Whose approach did you think was correct, and why?

10. The portrayal of the detective is colored by his own history on the island. Do you believe being a native makes it easier or more difficult to police a population?

———○———

Kelly loves meeting with book clubs—she's visited hundreds of groups. Email her to book a free in-person or Skype visit: kellysimmonswrites@gmail.com

Read on for an excerpt from Kelly Simmons's novel

ONE MORE DAY

Available now from Sourcebooks Landmark

MONDAY

Carrie Morgan's kidnapped son came back while she was at church.

Later, when she told a few fellow Episcopalians in Bronwyn, Pennsylvania, about this miracle—and she would, eventually, be brave enough to tell the whole story to a few new friends—they would point to this salient fact, gently insisting it was the linchpin. The cause, the effect. As if her faith had conjured a delicate simulacrum of her baby, truly ephemeral, wafer thin. She was taken aback by their steadfast view, the quietest version of fervor she'd ever witnessed. Most of the WASPs she knew—her mother, her in-laws—seemed able to take or leave their religion, abandoning it in favor of science, suspending church attendance for golf season. Or, as her Gran used to say, *as income rises, faith falls.* Indeed, when she pressed her own husband, John, asking him with tears in her eyes how he could have been an acolyte, how he could have been vice president of his youth group and *not believed* in what they both had seen with their own eyes, he had blinked at her and said, *Religion was sort of something we did, not something we believed.* An activity, a sport. A club.

Yet even after the whole week was finished and her deepest fears and faith confirmed, she would still shake her head and insist firmly that being at church when it had all been set in motion was merely a coincidence. She would try to convince everyone it was actually *ironic.*

Because she wasn't there at Saint David's—the soaring stone cathedral set high on a hill as if lording its wisdom over all the Philadelphia suburbs—kneeling, weeping, praying for her son's safe return; she'd stopped doing that months ago. No, she was mindlessly assembling brown boxes in the basement for their annual clothing drive and keeping track of her donated hours in the back of her mind so she could log it in her little notebook, as if she could hand over the evidence someday at the pearly gates.

It was early October, the part of the month still clinging to the grassy excess of summer, still warm enough that people were donating sweaters instead of coats, cottons instead of woolens. The boxes they packed were light. There were three other women: Anna, Joan, Libby. Carrie was stronger than the others and much younger. They were grateful to have her, happy to have someone sturdy and yet fragile. Someone who could be useful but who was still in great spiritual need herself. She looked so pretty and neat, her clothes always pulled together and her tortoiseshell hair perpetually shining in the stained glass light, but she still made mistakes, took risks, like a child. Defiant in her own way, headstrong as a toddler—they could tell by the set of her jaw. So much to learn! How often does a perfect volunteer like that come along?

It took a while, but Carrie had finally thrown herself back into volunteering. At first, she showed up whenever someone asked for volunteers—church, preschool, even bake sales at the nearby tennis club—trying not only to take her mind off her missing son, but also to create a new engine of purpose for her day. She hadn't just lost a child, she'd told her husband; she was a full-time mother—she'd lost her *job*. His face had twisted at that choice of words, and she'd been furious right back at him, in his face. *Oh, so I can't say that anymore? That raising a child is work? It wasn't all tickling and tossing the ball around, John!*

But more than the anger and the emptiness, there was the crushing sadness, sadness that was held back by some kind of societal seawall until it gathered fury and sloshed over everything. After a few breakdowns at school in front of women who managed to comfort her while also raising their eyebrows at the intensity of her sobs, she'd settled in at the church, where no one seemed to judge her. That she could go from competent to sniveling in a matter of seconds had no place at a school. Plus, she still looked so pretty when she cried. No reddening of the face, no smearing of mascara. *That's not real crying*, everyone whispered.

The children at school were always bubbling with questions, especially about adults who acted strangely. And the school was full of boys. Boys who didn't want to be stared at by a woman they didn't know who occasionally tried to touch their hair. The day she was asked to leave, the volunteer coordinator sat with Carrie in an empty science classroom, squeezed into the taut plastic chairs, and stared at the periodic table of elements while Carrie sobbed as if there were some chemical shorthand for what was happening to them all.

No, the church was further from the living, closer to the dead and the unforgivable. The church was where she belonged. The women there weren't like the young teachers and young mothers at school. They didn't believe anymore in perfect outfits, perfect homes, even perfect afternoons. They'd chipped their china; they'd buried their parents. They *knew*.

Some days, like that one, the hard work and convivial camaraderie did too good a job. Carrie almost forgot for whole blocks of time—hours sometimes—that Ben had been stolen from her car while she struggled with a parking meter outside Starbucks. Ripped from his car seat, leaving only a damp pacifier and one pale-blue sneaker. It haunted her for so long, wondering where the other shoe was, and then, suddenly, she could stop thinking about it. A miracle.

For weeks, the car smelled like Ben. John would come outside in the evenings and find her sitting in the backseat, breathing in the lost perfume of motherhood. The swallowed milk and damp hair, the aroma that lingered at his neck, around his ears. Even cranky, even tired, even with mud streaked on his face, Ben was never truly dirty. He smelled like milk and teething biscuits, wet paper straws and terry cloth bibs and fruity jelly. The finest combination of sour and sweet.

Months later, when John had her car cleaned and detailed, Carrie flew into a rage, pounding her fists against his chest, as if he'd been the parking attendant, as if he'd worn the uniform that made her scrabble through her purse for more money. As if he were the silver meter flashing a red flag demanding another quarter, starting the fight over twenty-five measly cents that had cost her everything. John held her, soothed her, made her dinner. Then he brought it up again. *We should move.* A few towns to the east, closer to his parents. So they could help them, so Carrie would have a change of scenery. And she shook her head so vigorously that the tears flew off her cheek. *We can't leave! What if Ben comes back?* And then, just like that, Ben did.

She floated between the boxes. Ben had been missing more than a year. It had been almost fifteen months, and only in the last few weeks had Carrie finally experienced the ability to separate from herself, suspended from her awful history, and forget—forget that she hadn't left her house or yard for weeks, that she'd been almost catatonic; forget that she once heard John telling his mother on the phone, *It's like she was taken the same day he was.*

She forgot how she sat in the dark, rewinding Ben's crib mobile over and over again, the path of the stuffed stars and quilted moon circling for hours above her head, the lullaby always in her ears. John had finally taken it down and told her the mechanism had burned, the battery sparking. She'd found it, days later, in the basement, tucked inside a pail full of rags. Hiding the evidence. Proof that John couldn't take it; he just couldn't take it anymore. But she could. She could take it forever. She'd come upstairs with the mobile, wagging it in his face, telling him, *Hang it back up, damn it! Now!*

"Sometimes I think you want to stay sad," John had said as he'd grabbed it out of her hand. "Like you deserve it or something."

And she'd gone in the bathroom and whispered to the mirror, "Maybe I do."

But after so much time, the tasks she'd assigned herself sometimes took over, as they were supposed to, distracting her, and then— realizing they'd done so—threw her into guilt. Distraction, guilt, distraction. But sometimes, for a few hours, that distraction brought a level of comfort. Not happiness exactly, but something close.

She moved lightly, fluidly, as empty people tend to do. A ghost in a coral cotton sweater and gray lululemon tennis skirt, moving through the dusty corridors, someone with nothing, carrying other people's cast-off things. If there had been baby clothes in a bag in that narrow basement, she would have thought of Ben, surely. If, while driving there, she had passed the new groomed playground, all curved edges and bright colors and wood chips, and seen a ball being kicked across the short, mowed grass, she would have ached inside. His first words, *ball* and *bat*, and not, as she loved to joke, what she kept training him to say: "Thank you, Mommy." But instead of dwelling on her boy, she worked swiftly while discussing innocuous subjects like golf. Whether Libby should start playing with her husband during his impending retirement. Anna sharing her belief that several ladies in the congregation cheated on their scores regularly.

"I'm so glad you're feeling better," Libby said as they walked out to the parking lot. She squeezed Carrie's hand tightly, then held it as an older sister might as they stood next to Libby's dusty, dog-hair-filled Subaru wagon. Libby had always been Carrie's favorite person at the church. She came from one of the wealthiest Philadelphia families—it was embedded in her monogram forever, K for *Kelly*, a letter that stood wider than all the others, strong enough to withstand gossip, to live on reputation alone—but she lived her life like she had no money or pedigree at all. The oldest car in the church parking lot. Straight, blunt hair that belied her soft heart. Mothballs the only perfume she ever wore.

Libby couldn't help smiling when she was around Carrie and her husband, John. It was as if, by knowing them, she caught a glimpse of how her own daughter's life might have turned out if she hadn't been killed in a car accident at sixteen. Pious, hardworking, organized, Mary, her daughter, had been blonder, shorter, slighter, but she was just as strong and openhearted.

Libby had finally renovated Mary's old bedroom a few years ago and had given one of Mary's needlepoint belts to Carrie. Carrie had run her fingers over the tiny knots and *x*'s with wonder, like she was reading Braille, parsing the meaning of the design, the small whales and gulls and anchors. Libby loved seeing it, peeking out beneath the bottom of Carrie's coral sweater, threaded through the belt loops of her tennis skirt.

"How can you tell I'm feeling better?" Carrie asked.

"Oh, it's plain as day."

"Because you haven't found me curled up in the basement bathroom with tissues stuffed up my nose in a while?"

"Well, yes." Libby laughed.

"They really should invent a product for frequent criers whose noses run. Like a nose tampon. There's probably a huge market for it."

"See, that's what I mean—making a joke again. There's a... lightness to you lately."

Carrie returned Libby's smile. Libby always laughed at Carrie's quips. In high school, the girls her own age had never seemed to understand her sense of humor. She'd make a comment or observation in class, and the teacher would smile, but the students would look at her like she was speaking a foreign language.

Libby got in her car and pretended to fiddle with something in her purse. She sneaked glances toward Carrie as she walked to her car, closed the door, turned on her engine. Carrie drove past Libby, waving again.

Slivers of sun still shone stubbornly on the speckled alders dotting both sides of the creek in the distance. But slate-bottomed clouds hung heavy above the green oaks and lindens circling the parking lot, shading Libby's car.

Libby watched Carrie a long time, till she was out of sight, then did something she only felt a bit guilty about. She sent a two-word text: *En route*. She thought it was sweet that Carrie's husband worried about her. Libby was a slow texter, with large calloused thumbs from gardening, and as she pecked out the message with her head bent down, another car sprang to life in the parking lot. It pulled out of a far corner, headed in the same direction as Carrie's.

Carrie took the shorter way home, via Route 30. She glanced at the rearview mirror a dozen times, but it was only to smile at the bobbing blue sneaker, Ben's remaining sneaker, that hung there. Like Dr. Kenney had suggested, she took it out of the drawer where she'd been keeping it and tried to consider it a good luck charm. But the swaying shoe mesmerized like a hypnotist's watch, and she never saw the car lurking half a block behind her, turning when she turned, veering when she veered. Even if she had noticed, it never would have occurred to her that something was amiss. Everyone on the edge of the Main Line drove the same predictable routes. She didn't worry. It had been a week since Detective Nolan came over to ask her "one more thing" that sounded innocuous but probably wasn't, days since she'd fumed to her mother that no one ever asked John more questions, only her. He'd been in Ardmore that day too, hadn't he? Said he went out for a run after lunch, but had anyone tracked down his route, asked for the DNA on his sweaty clothes? What would they say if they knew how jealous he'd been in college, how he'd followed Carrie when she went alone to fund-raisers or parties and watched as she went inside? But she didn't think about this. And it had been hours, two at least, since she had thought about her son. Because she was getting better. She was coming back to life. *She was.*

She took the last winding curves of Sugarland Road, passing the moss-dappled houses in the distance, the endless driveways up green hills, everything weathered and nothing glittery, no agate twinkling between the low fieldstone walls. She turned onto her street, a dark macadam slash flanked by piles of faux stone. She pulled into the abbreviated driveway and got out of her car. She opened her hollow red front door, and she heard it then, that babbling half language only babies and toddlers know. The sounds she wished she had recorded more of, remembered better, once they were gone. She put her hand up to her mouth and walked slowly up the stairs. She sniffed the air for traces of him—powder, shampoo—but smelled something that reminded her of a soiled diaper. The sounds grew louder, unmistakable, and she couldn't decide if she was thrilled—or deeply afraid.

A Conversation with the Author

There are five first-person points of view in the book. How did you arrive at that approach, and how did you differentiate the character voices?

Well, originally there were more! My editor, quite wisely, asked me to narrow and focus them, choosing the most important voices. The variety of genders, ages, dialects, and backgrounds helped me ground them, and I tried to make their actions and dialogue distinct without being stereotypical or obvious or employing any kind of high-wire stylized writerly crap. Writer's stunts usually feel like bad radio commercials you want to mute!

The Nantucket setting seems integral to the plot. How much research did you do on this area of the country? Did you ever consider setting it somewhere else? If so, why?

I'm sure there are other places where similar tensions simmer beneath the surface, but I have been carefully observing Nantucket for many years, having spent all or part of each summer on the island for more than twenty years. I cannot imagine setting it anywhere else. That being said, despite my familiarity, I had to do a lot of research about all kinds of things: vegetation, weather, history—there were so many things I did not know!

As this novel goes to press, there are eerie parallels between the hate crimes in the book to hate crimes in the United States. How do you feel about that?

Sick. Sad. And astonished that something I conjured years ago, and that frankly seemed almost unbelievable at one time, has become all too real.

This is your second book that focuses on religious differences. Any particular reason you are interested in that topic?

I think because I'm not religious that I find religious zeal and passion particularly fascinating. And religious prejudice pretty much unfathomable.

It could be argued that every single character in this novel, from age twelve to seventy, behaves badly. Why did you choose to do this, and what type of bad behavior do you relate to most?

Okay, that question made me laugh—and made me realize how much trouble I could get into here! One of the things I really sought to showcase in this book is how seemingly small betrayals can have devastating consequences, and how larger criminal acts can almost make sense, when you put them in context. As for the second half of the question, I relate, on the whole, to Tripp joyfully throwing caution to the wind. I love it when people don't care what other people think!

Police notes and police reports are sprinkled throughout the book. What made you choose this approach?

I thought it was a simple but fun way to keep the police presence in the book without turning it into a crime novel, because it is, at its core, a family novel.

The stresses of raising children while managing elderly parents collide to great effect in this novel. Do you have some direct life experience with this?

My husband and I have weathered a pretty full spectrum of experiences with our parents—surprising illnesses, sudden death, lingering and heartbreaking declines—all while raising three daughters. I have nothing but compassion for families going through this.

What are you working on next? More religious zeal and bad behavior?

Bad behavior always! I'm currently tinkering with a novel about a fugitive mom trying to reconnect with her long-lost sister. See? Bad mom. Fugitive.

Have more questions? Learn more at kellysimmonsbooks.com

Acknowledgments

No author is an island. Even when writing a book about an island. I'm grateful to my family and friends who tolerate my obsessions, my absurd observations, and my constant note-taking. And to my agent, Anne Bohner, and the entire team at Sourcebooks—Anna, Shana, Lathea, and so many others in all departments. Thank you to all the lovely book clubs and bookstores who have welcomed me. And I owe an enormous debt to my vibrant, supportive community of fellow authors—the Liars Club and Writers Coffeehouse gang, the Tall Poppy Writers, the Main Line Writers Group That Never Writes, the Helveticats, Natasha & Sasha. Hugs. Kisses. Beer.

About the Author

Photo credit: Bill Ecklund

Kelly Simmons is the author of *One More Day*, *Standing Still*, and *The Bird House*. She is a former journalist and advertising creative director who divides her time between writing, teaching, public speaking, vacuuming up dog hair, and refereeing her three daughters. She's a member of WFWA, the Tall Poppy Writers, and the Liars Club, and teaches at Drexel University's Storylab. Visit her website at kellysimmonsbooks.com.